JAKE MADDOX

GRAPH

RUNNING OVERLOAD

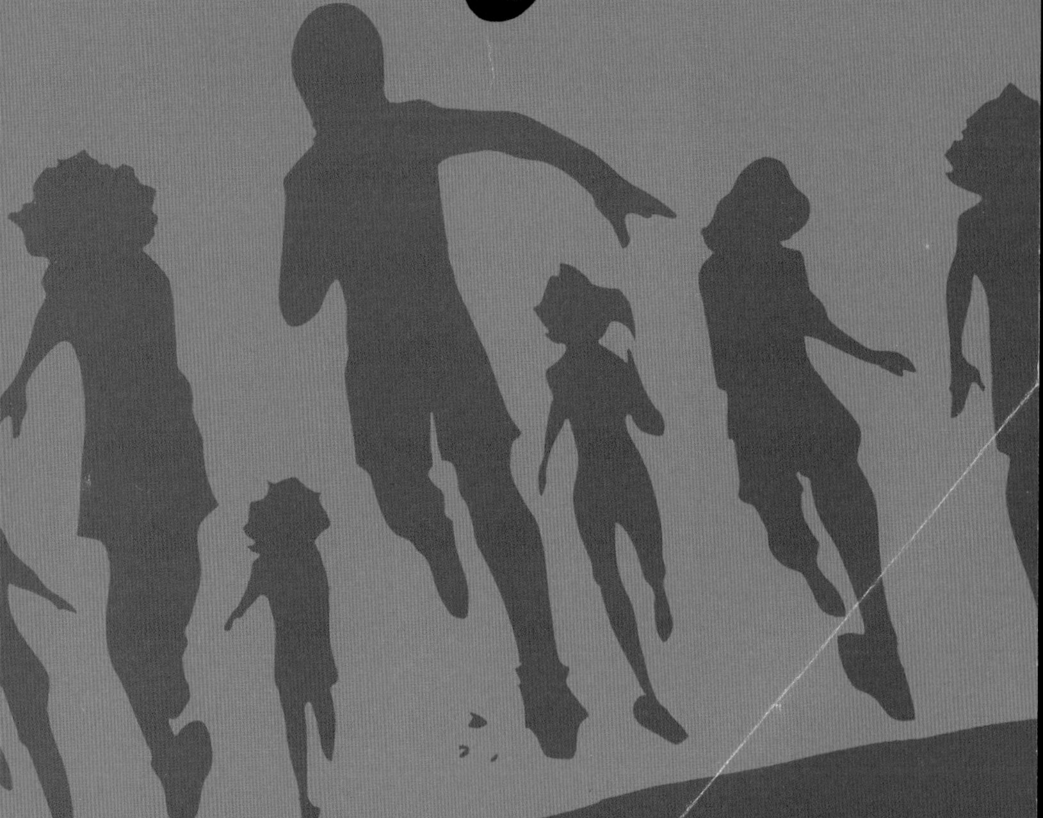

STONE ARCH BOOKS
a capstone imprint

JAKE MADDOX
GRAPHIC NOVELS

Published by Stone Arch Books,
an imprint of Capstone.
1710 Roe Crest Drive
North Mankato, Minnesota 56003
www.capstonepub.com

Copyright © 2020 by Capstone. All rights reserved.
No part of this publication may be reproduced in
whole or in part, or stored in a retrieval system, or
transmitted in any form or by any means, electronic,
mechanical, photocopying, recording, or otherwise,
without written permission of the publisher.

Library of Congress Cataloging-in-Publication Data
is available on the Library of Congress website.

ISBN: 978-1-4965-8377-2 (library binding)
ISBN: 978-1-4965-8456-4 (paperback)
ISBN: 978-1-4965-8382-6 (ebook PDF)

Summary: Eighth grader Nimo Mohamed has made
the varsity cross-country team, and she's determined
to keep up with the older girls. She's training harder
than ever—maybe too hard. Because soon the
runner's grades are tumbling, her times are slipping,
and her body is completely exhausted. Can Nimo
learn to pace herself and stop this running overload?

Designed by Brann Garvey

Printed in the United States of America.
PA100

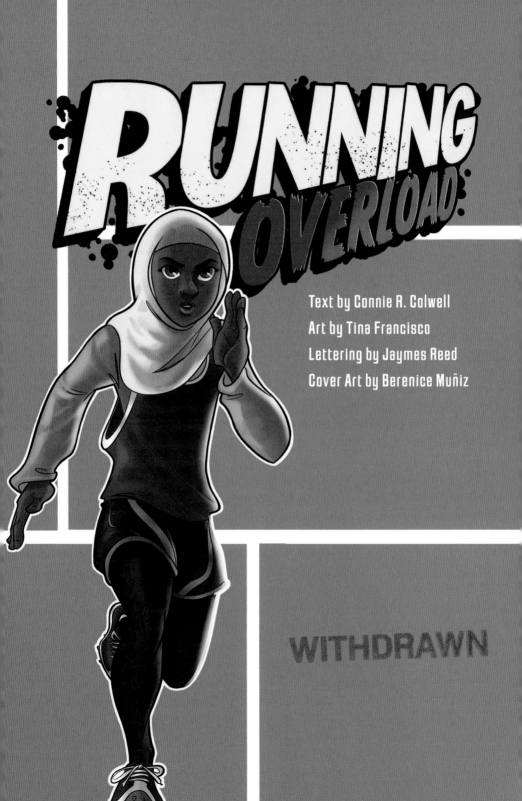

RUNNING OVERLOAD

Text by Connie R. Colwell

Art by Tina Francisco

Lettering by Jaymes Reed

Cover Art by Berenice Muñiz

WITHDRAWN

STARTING LINEUP

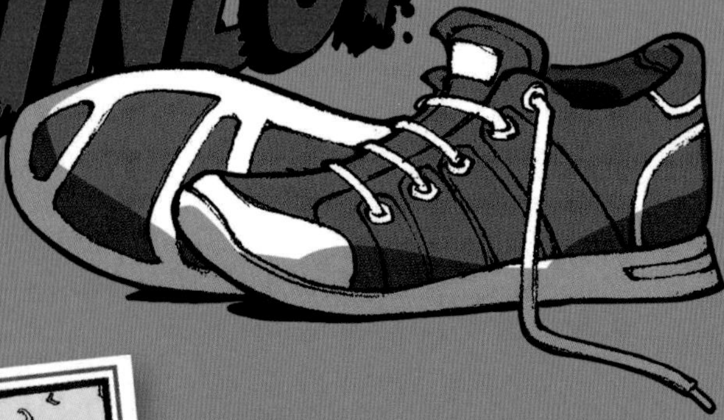

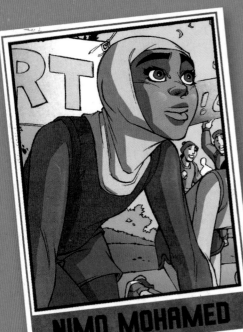

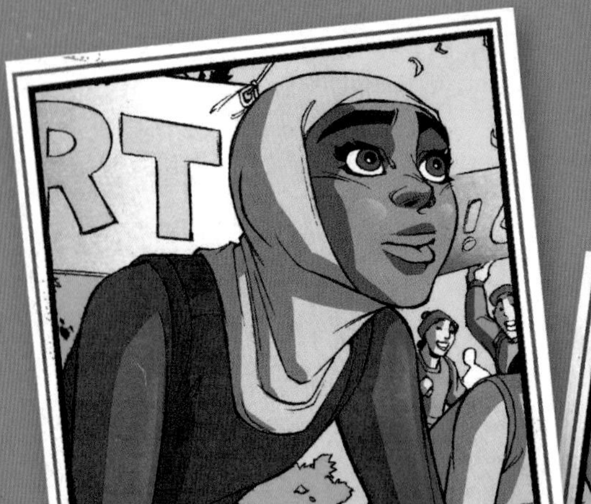
NIMO MOHAMED

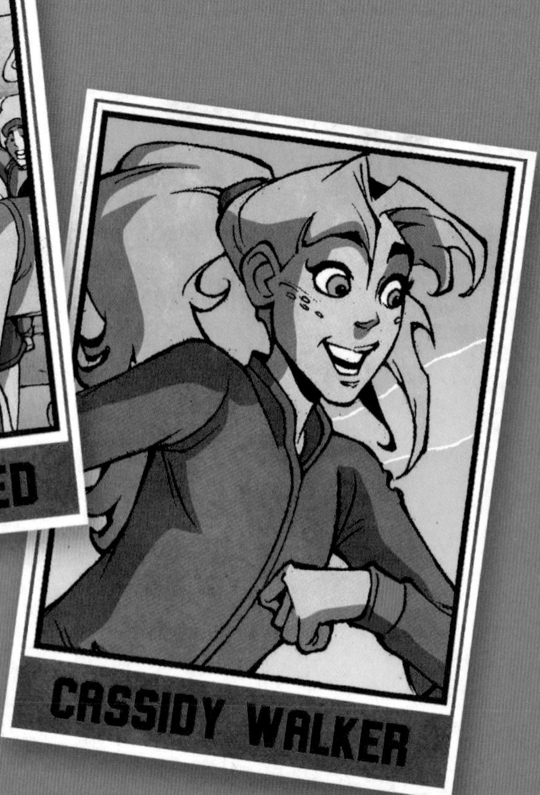
CASSIDY WALKER

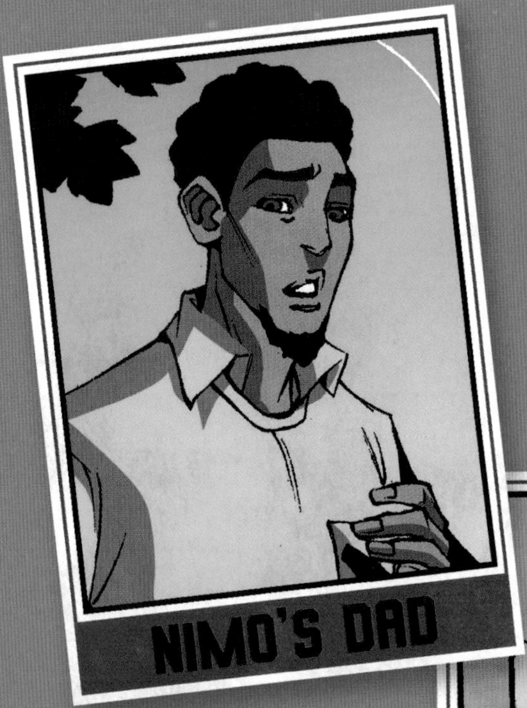
NIMO'S DAD

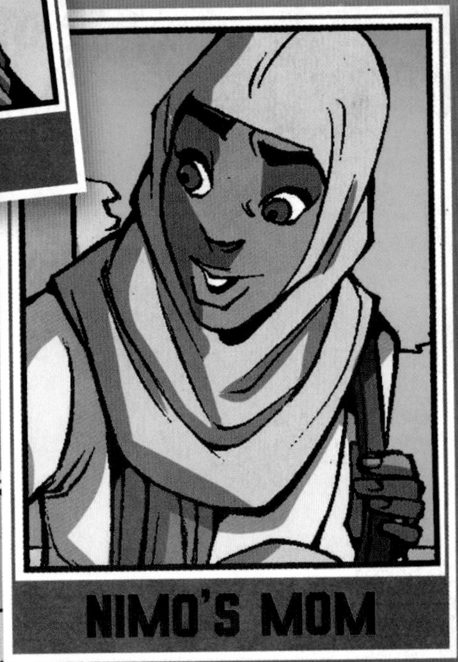
NIMO'S MOM

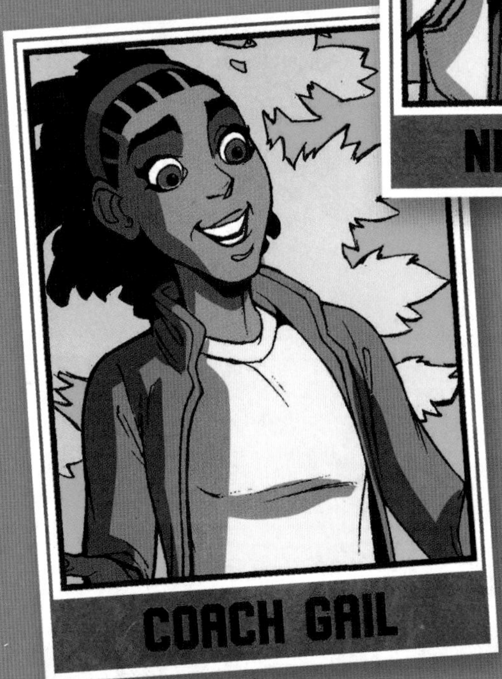
COACH GAIL

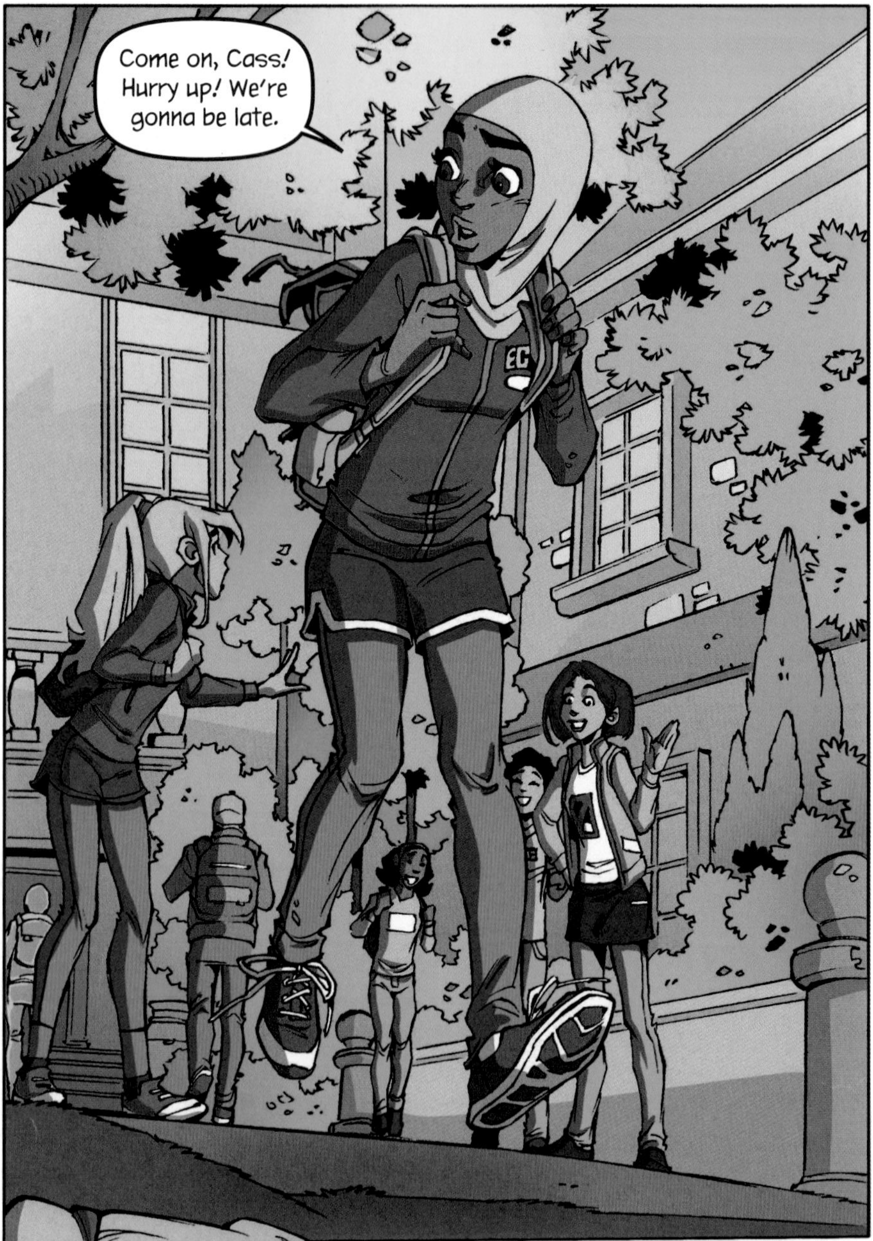
Come on, Cass! Hurry up! We're gonna be late.
EC

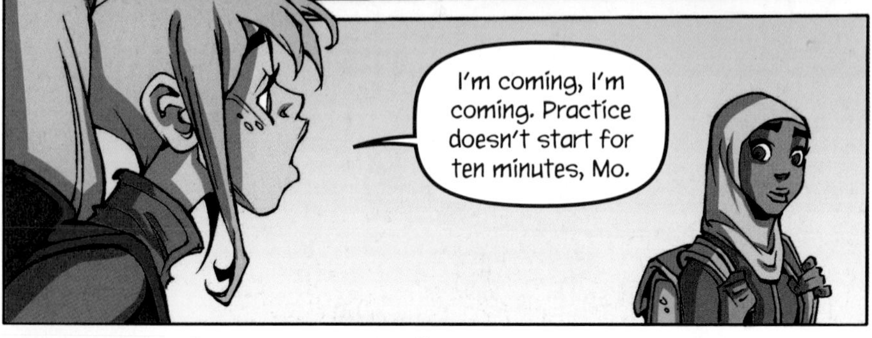
I'm coming, I'm coming. Practice doesn't start for ten minutes, Mo.

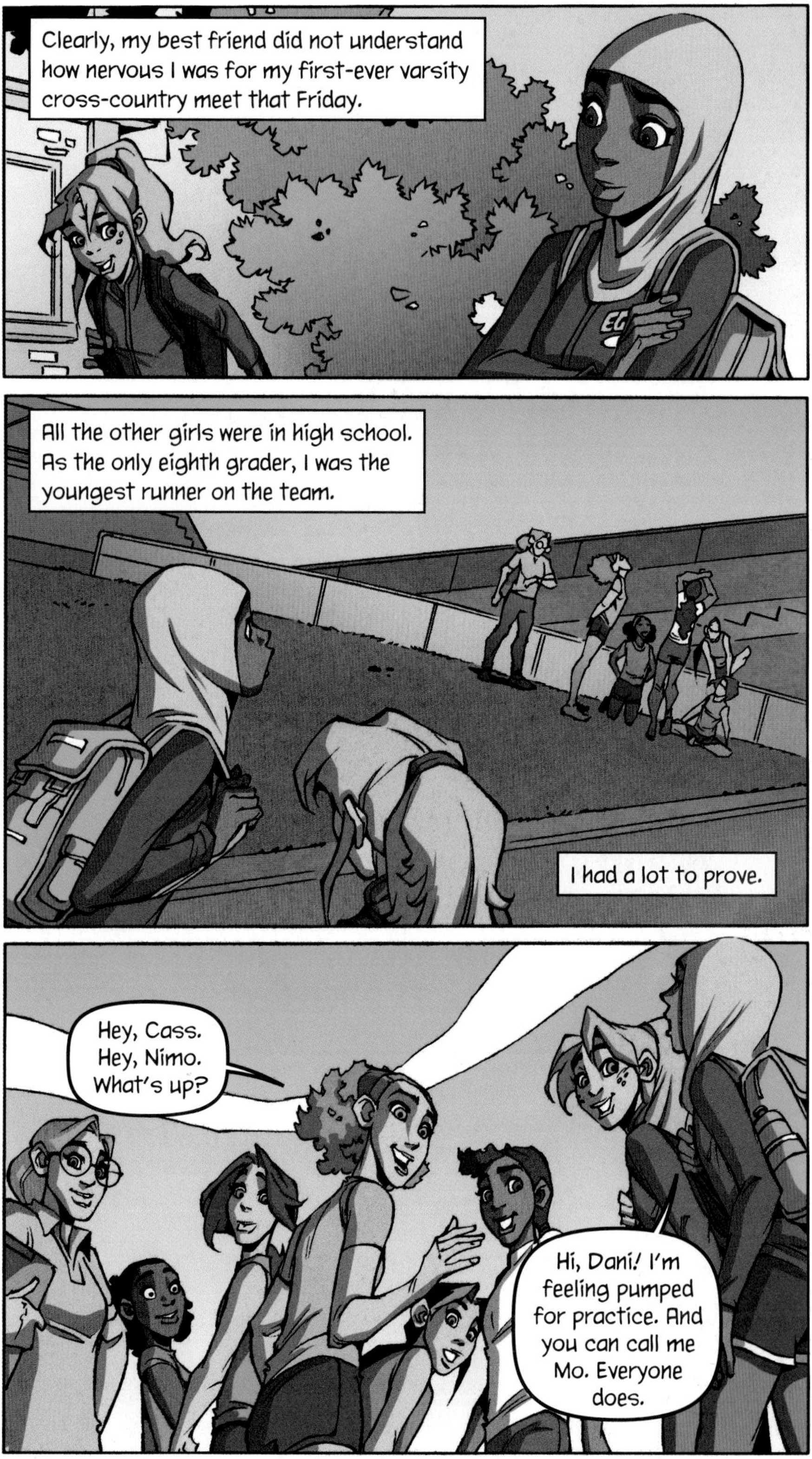
Clearly, my best friend did not understand how nervous I was for my first-ever varsity cross-country meet that Friday.
All the other girls were in high school. As the only eighth grader, I was the youngest runner on the team.
I had a lot to prove.
Hey, Cass. Hey, Nimo. What's up?
Hi, Dani! I'm feeling pumped for practice. And you can call me Mo. Everyone does.

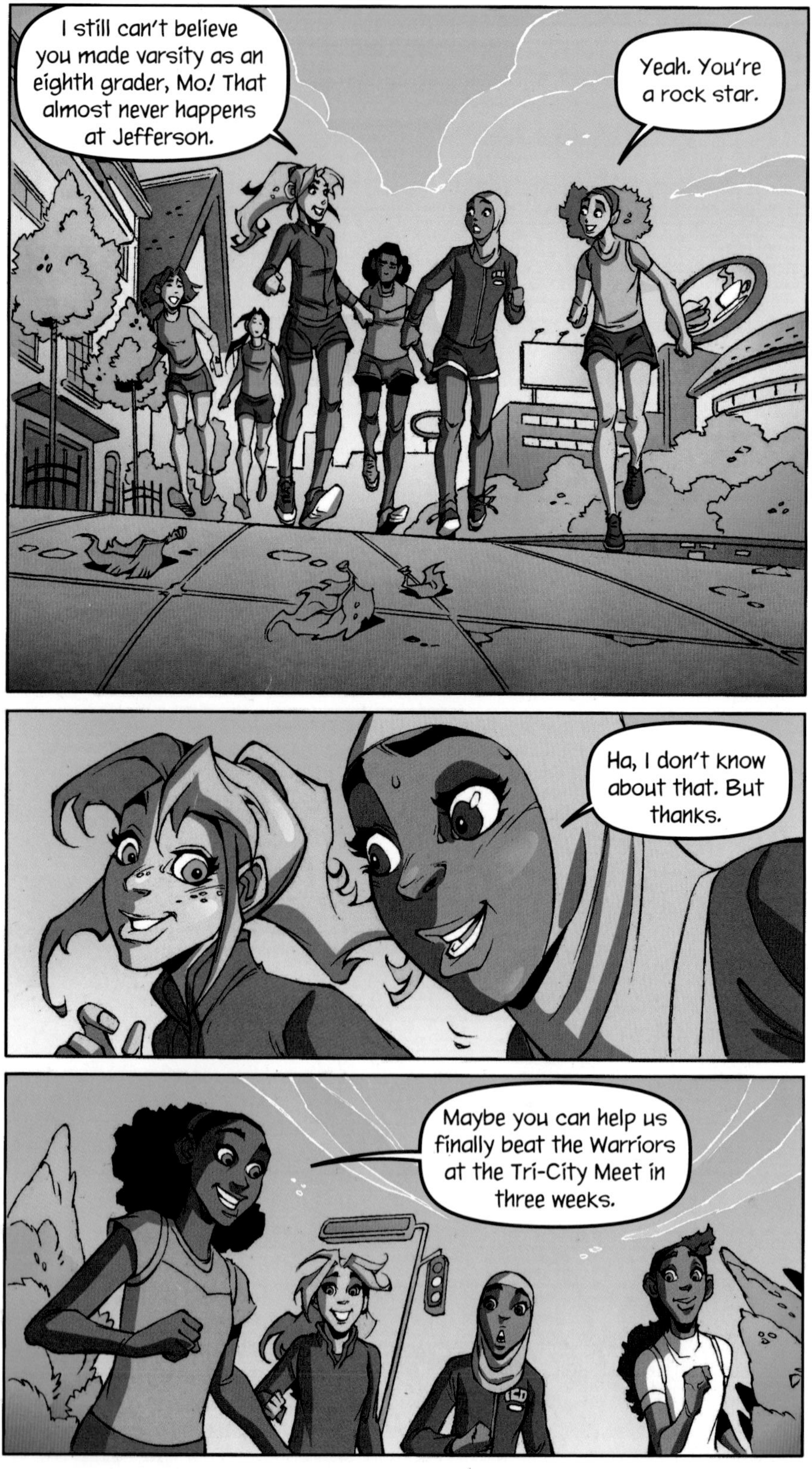
I still can't believe you made varsity as an eighth grader, Mo! That almost never happens at Jefferson.
Yeah. You're a rock star.
Ha, I don't know about that. But thanks.
Maybe you can help us finally beat the Warriors at the Tri-City Meet in three weeks.

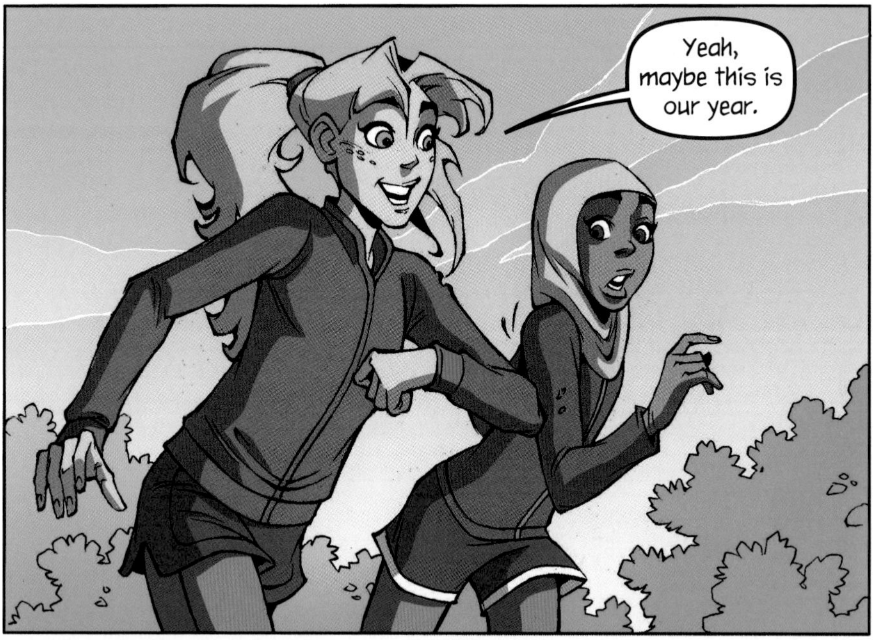
Yeah, maybe this is our year.

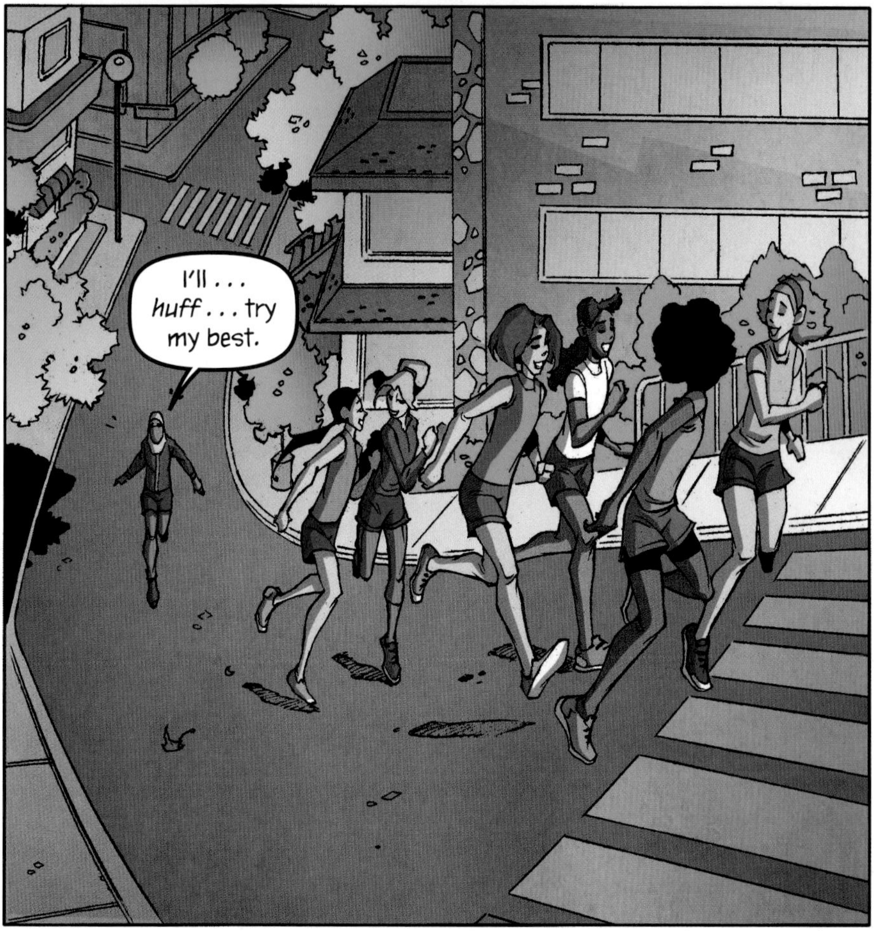
I'll . . . *huff* . . . try my best.

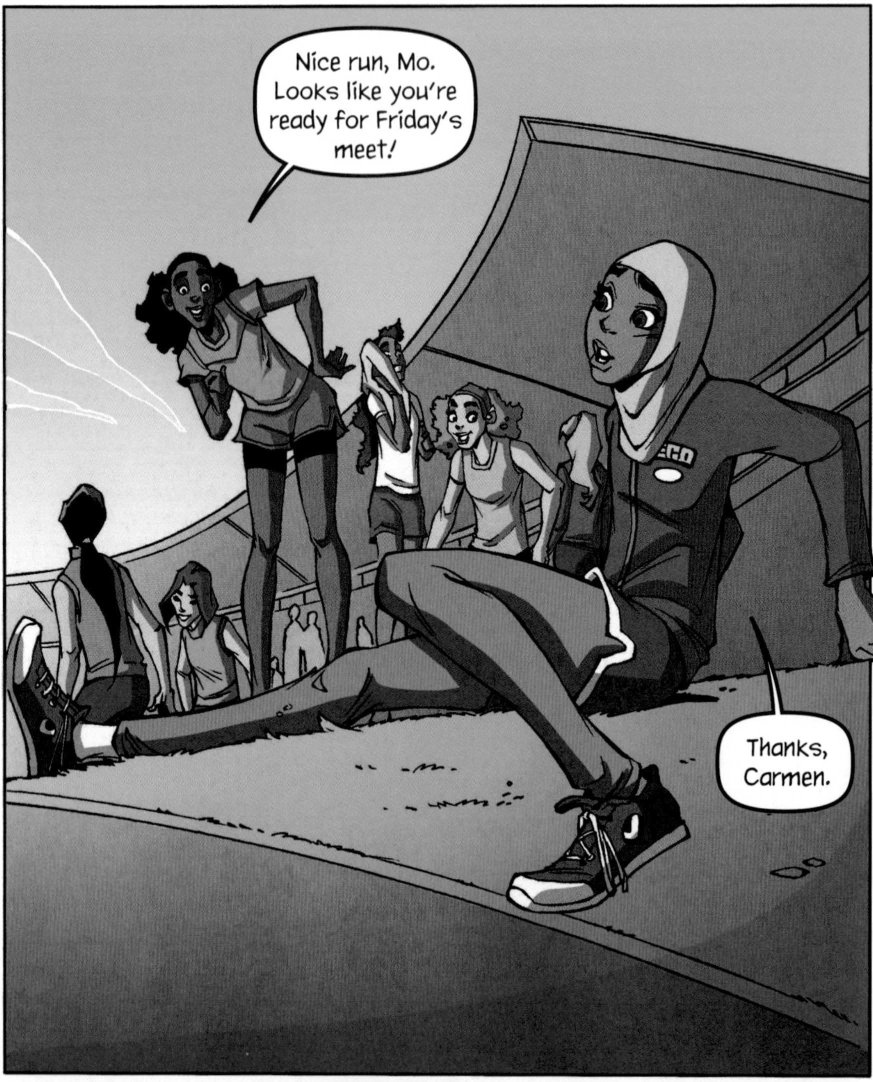
Nice run, Mo. Looks like you're ready for Friday's meet!
Thanks, Carmen.

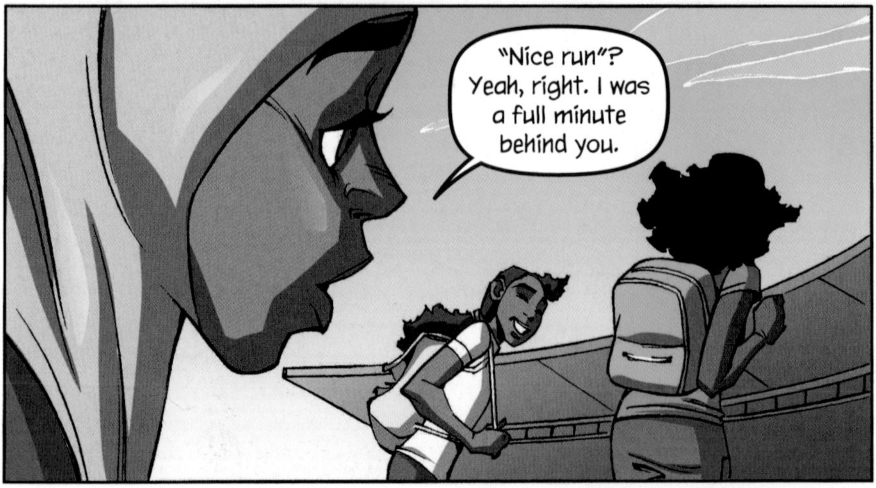
"Nice run"? Yeah, right. I was a full minute behind you.

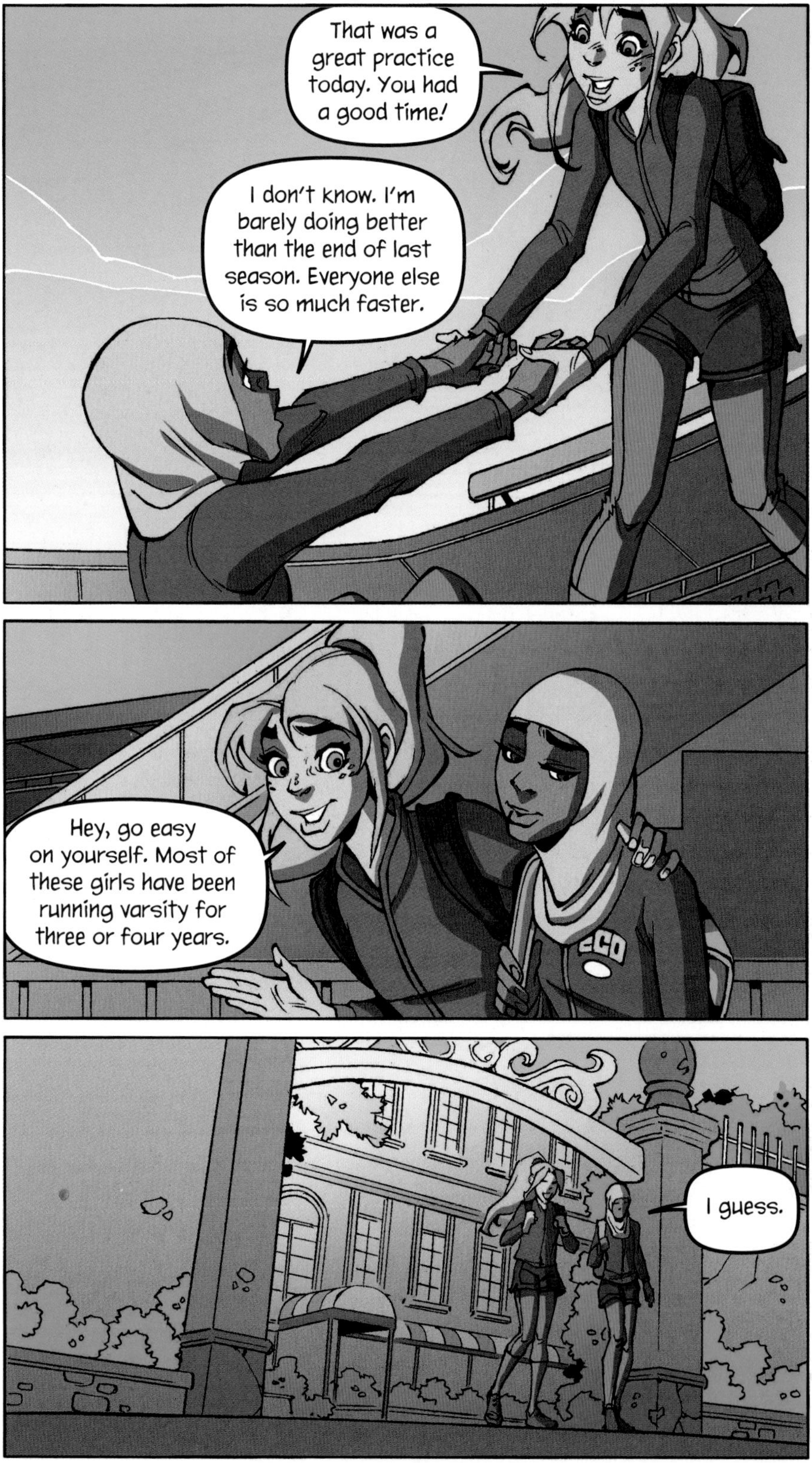
That was a great practice today. You had a good time!
I don't know. I'm barely doing better than the end of last season. Everyone else is so much faster.
Hey, go easy on yourself. Most of these girls have been running varsity for three or four years.
I guess.

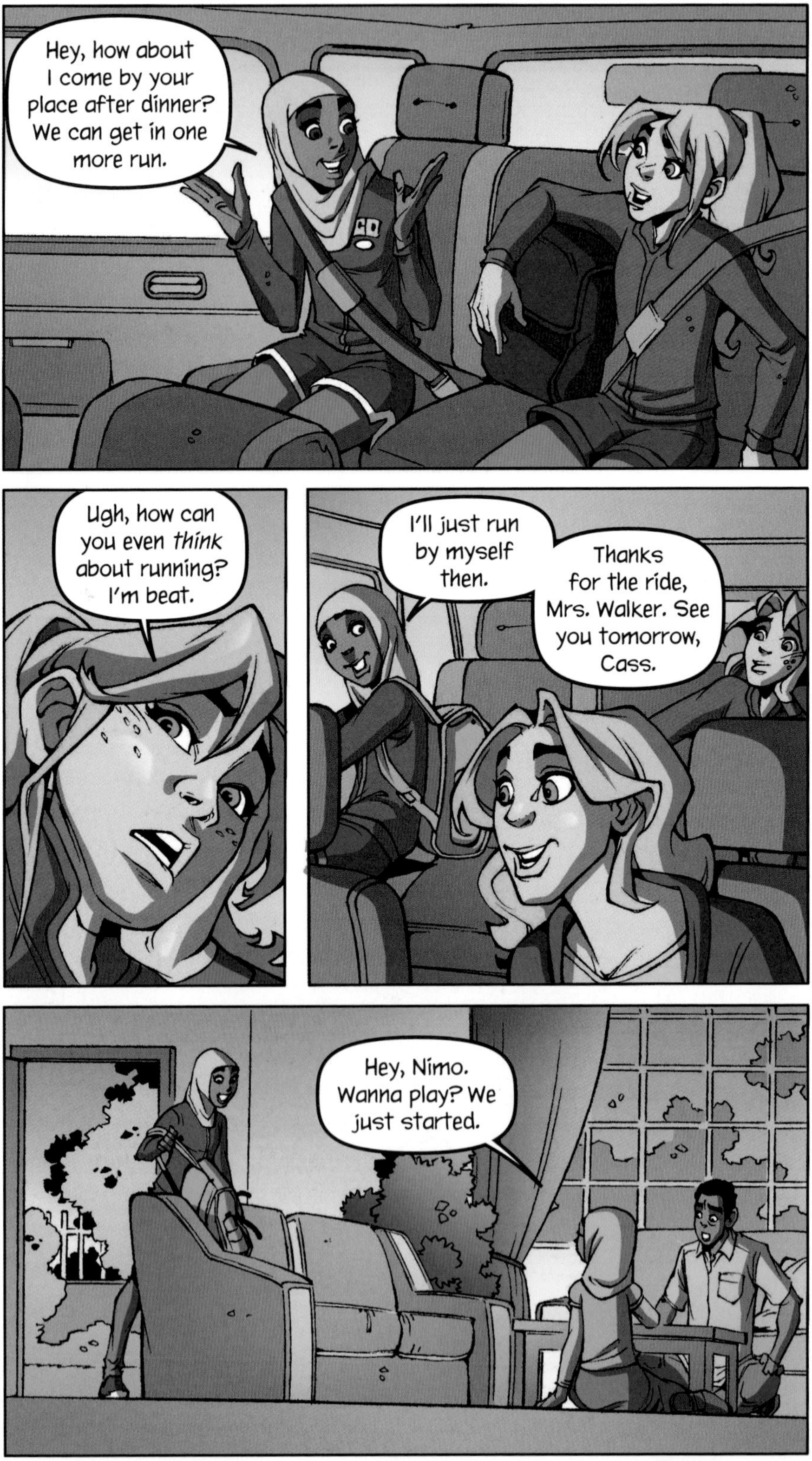
Hey, how about I come by your place after dinner? We can get in one more run.
Ugh, how can you even *think* about running? I'm beat.
I'll just run by myself then.
Thanks for the ride, Mrs. Walker. See you tomorrow, Cass.
Hey, Nimo. Wanna play? We just started.

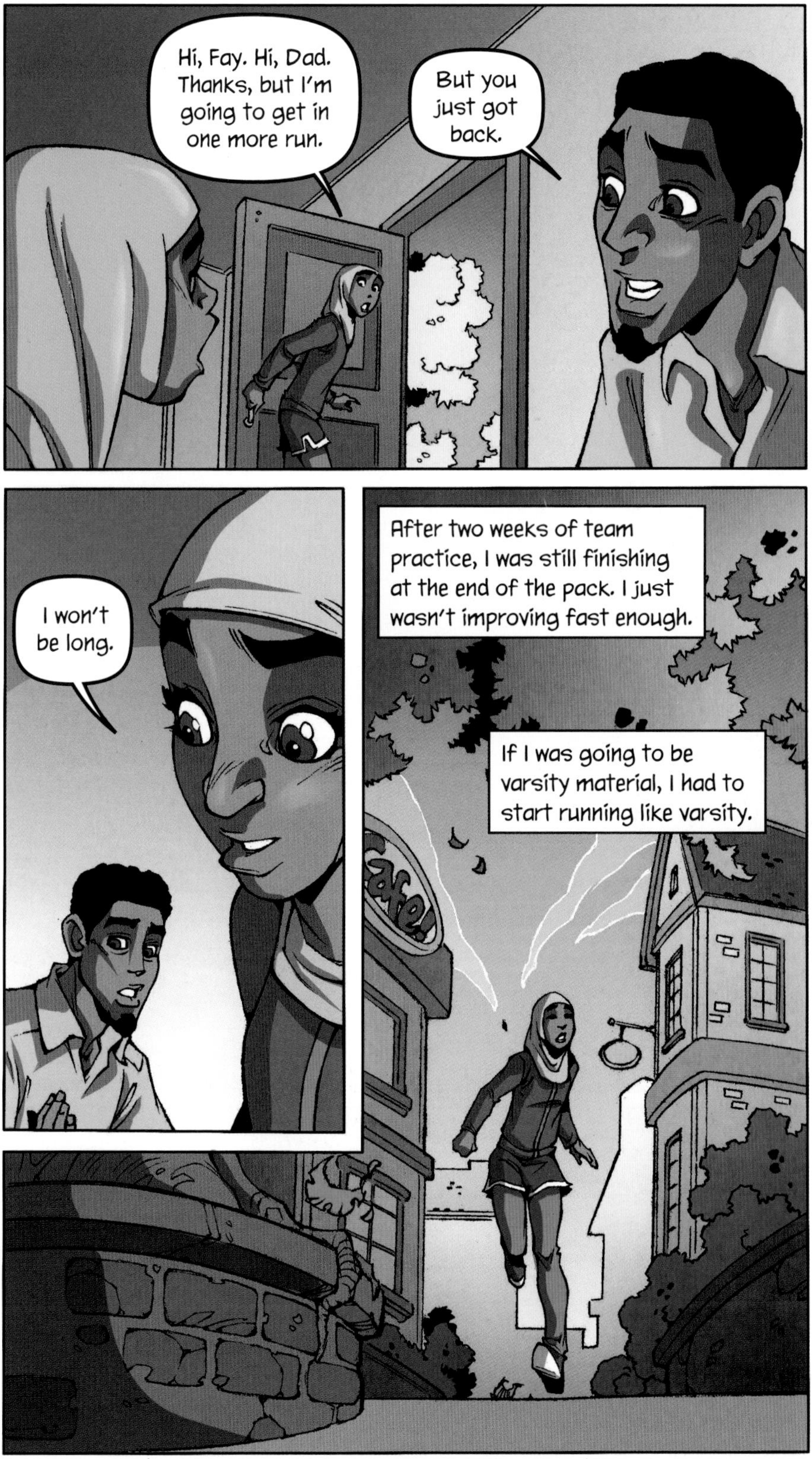
Hi, Fay. Hi, Dad. Thanks, but I'm going to get in one more run.
But you just got back.
I won't be long.
After two weeks of team practice, I was still finishing at the end of the pack. I just wasn't improving fast enough.
If I was going to be varsity material, I had to start running like varsity.

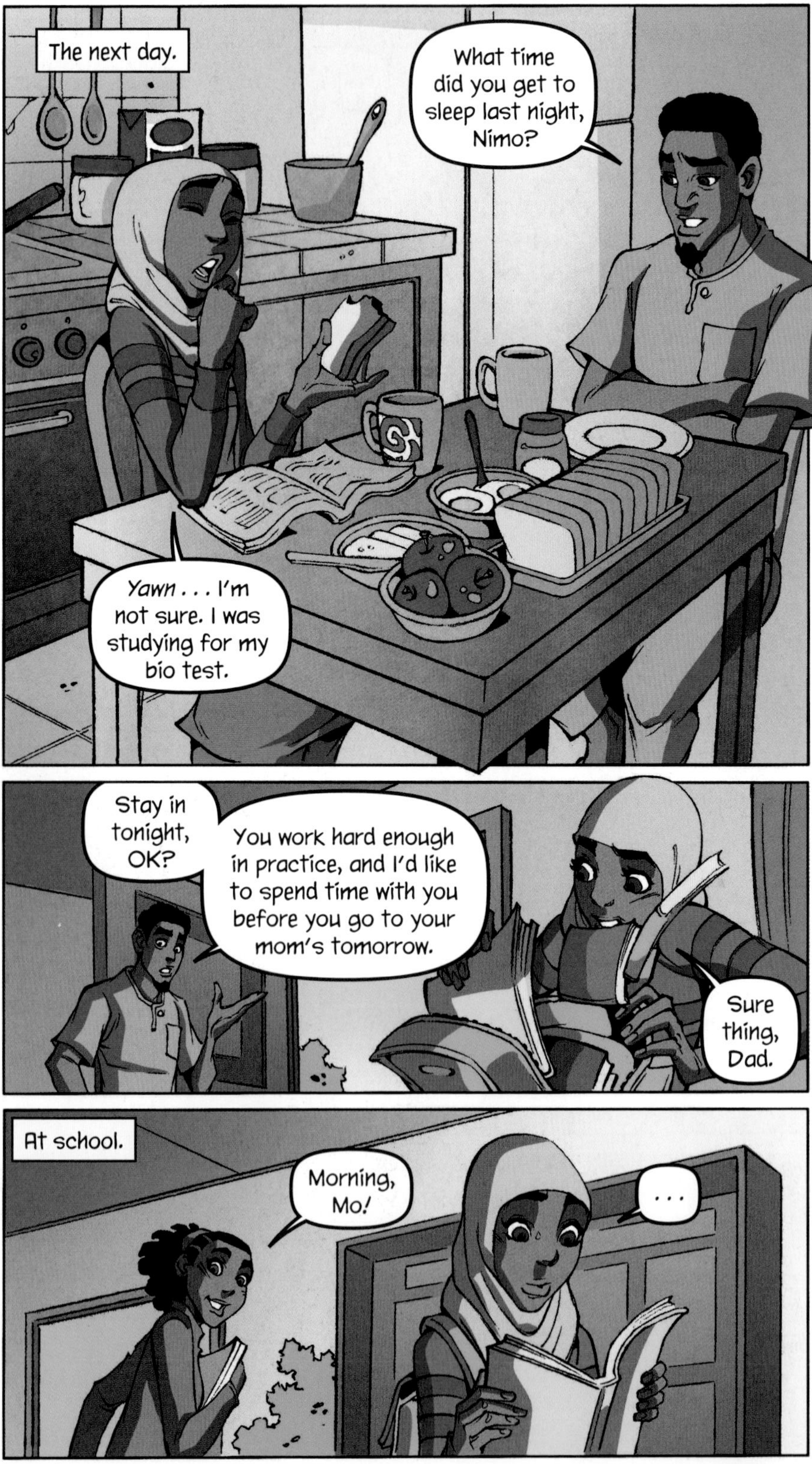
The next day.
What time did you get to sleep last night, Nimo?
Yawn . . . I'm not sure. I was studying for my bio test.
Stay in tonight, OK?
You work hard enough in practice, and I'd like to spend time with you before you go to your mom's tomorrow.
Sure thing, Dad.
At school.
Morning, Mo!
. . .

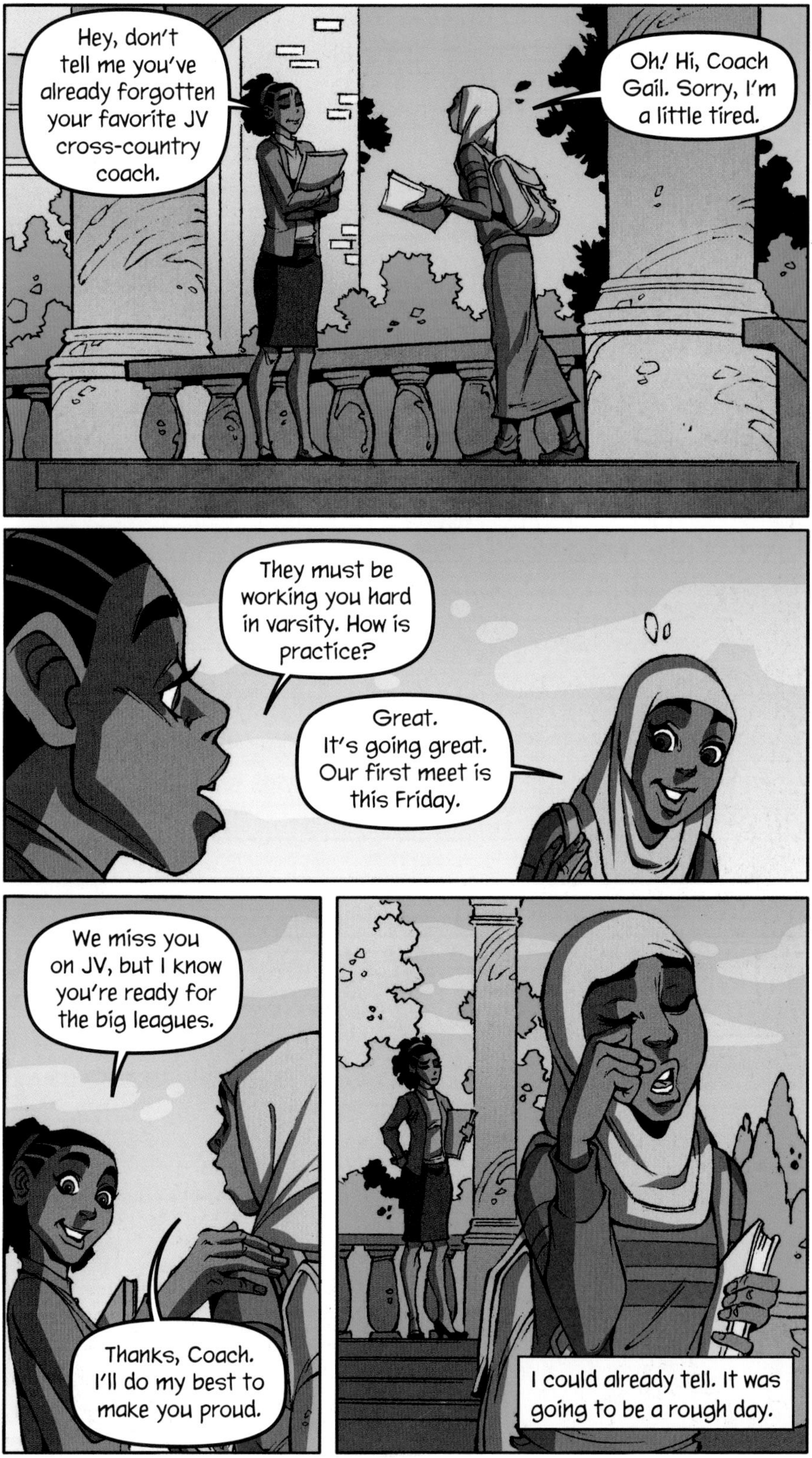
Hey, don't tell me you've already forgotten your favorite JV cross-country coach.
Oh! Hi, Coach Gail. Sorry, I'm a little tired.
They must be working you hard in varsity. How is practice?
Great. It's going great. Our first meet is this Friday.
We miss you on JV, but I know you're ready for the big leagues.
Thanks, Coach. I'll do my best to make you proud.
I could already tell. It was going to be a rough day.

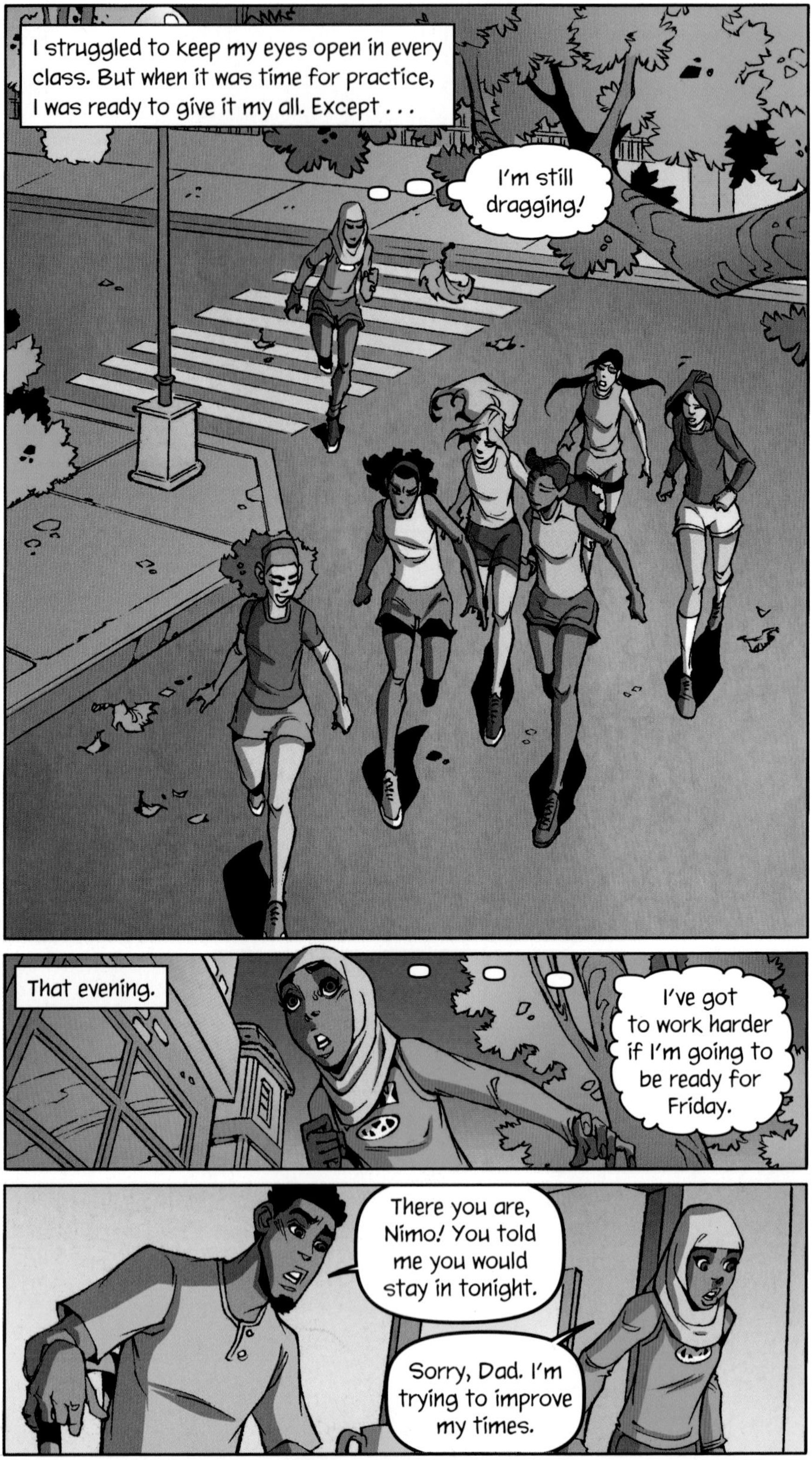
I struggled to keep my eyes open in every class. But when it was time for practice, I was ready to give it my all. Except . . .
I'm still dragging!
That evening.
I've got to work harder if I'm going to be ready for Friday.
There you are, Nimo! You told me you would stay in tonight.
Sorry, Dad. I'm trying to improve my times.

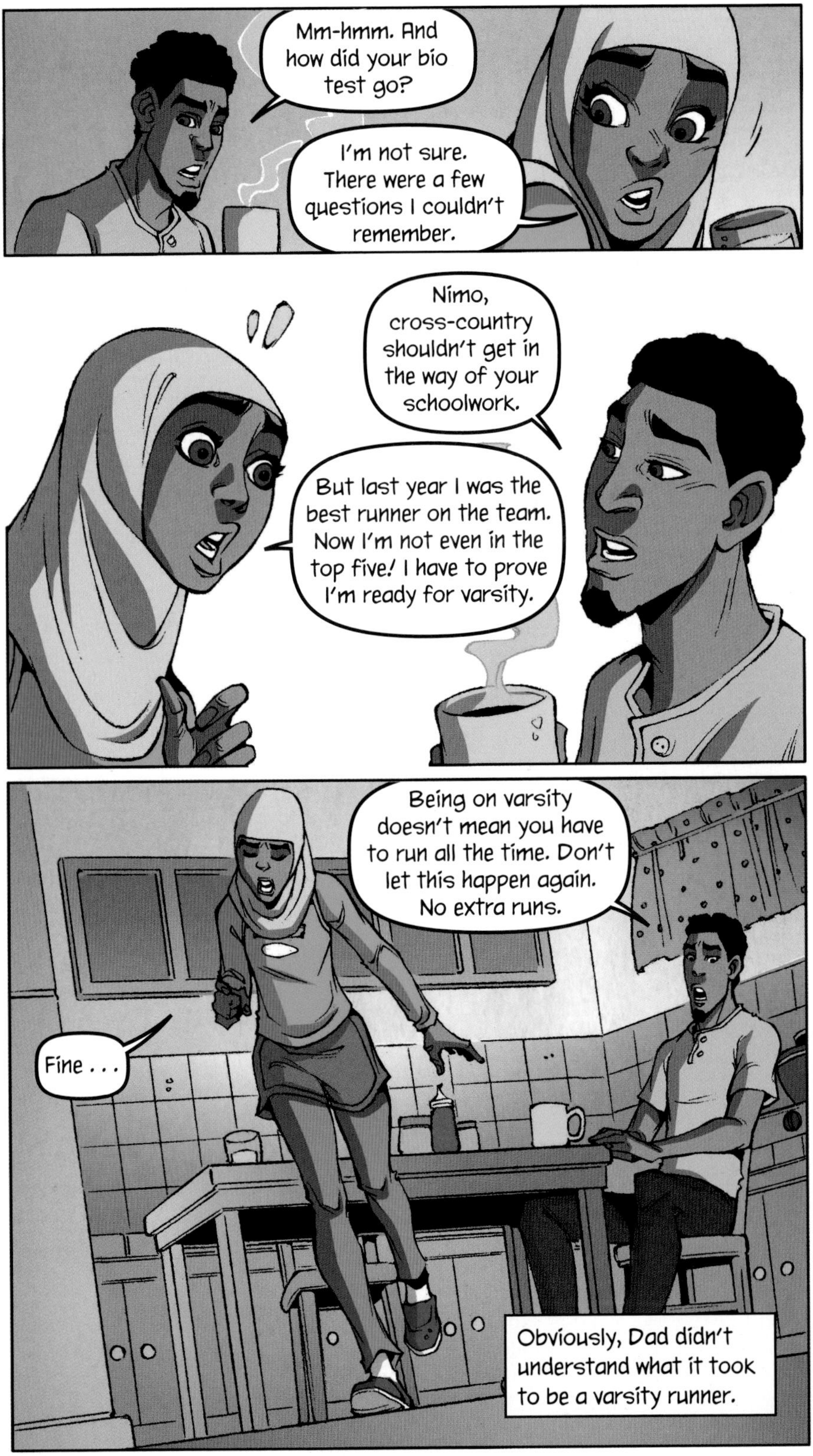
Mm-hmm. And how did your bio test go?
I'm not sure. There were a few questions I couldn't remember.
Nimo, cross-country shouldn't get in the way of your schoolwork.
But last year I was the best runner on the team. Now I'm not even in the top five! I have to prove I'm ready for varsity.
Being on varsity doesn't mean you have to run all the time. Don't let this happen again. No extra runs.
Fine . . .
Obviously, Dad didn't understand what it took to be a varsity runner.

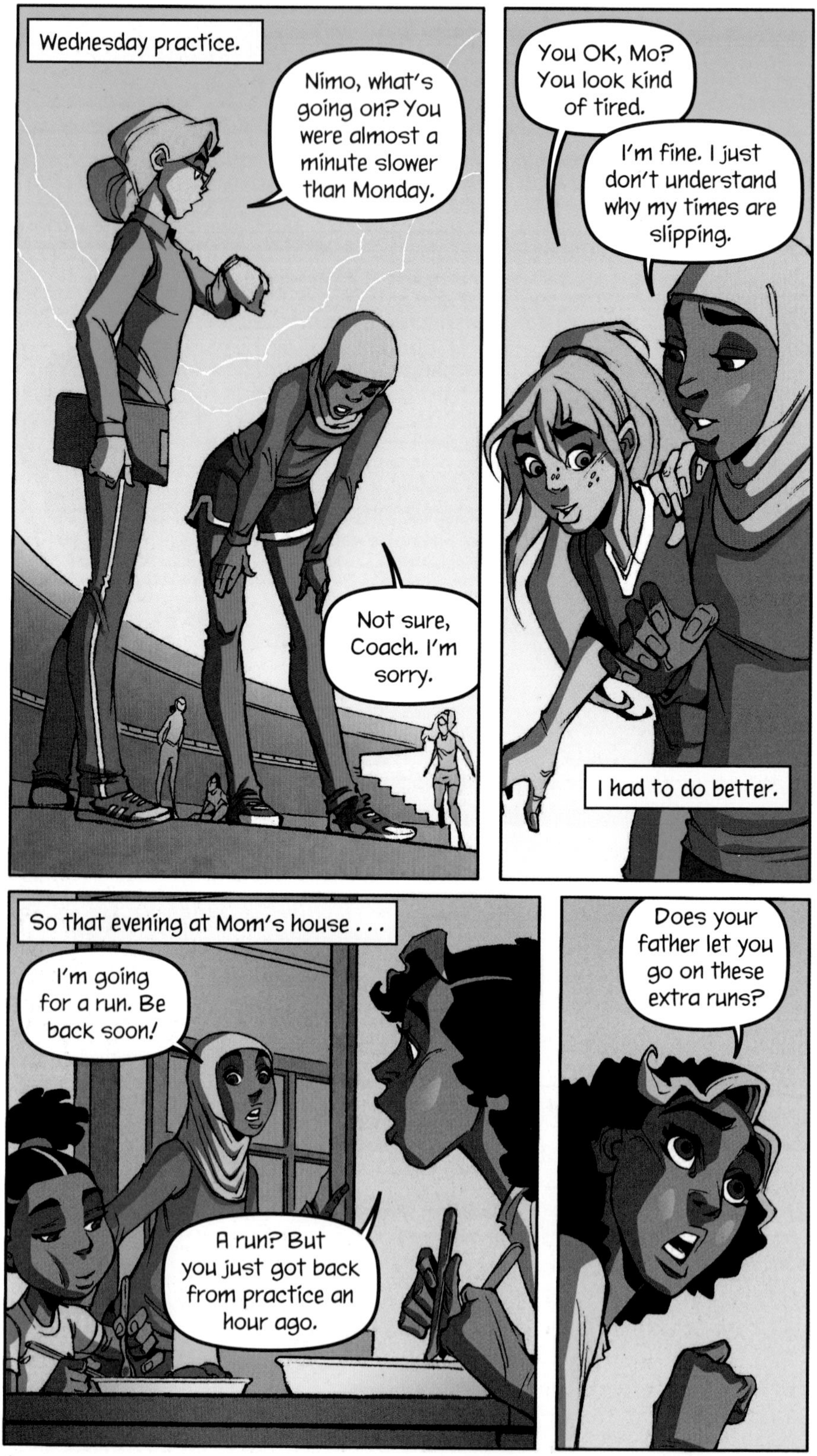
Wednesday practice.
Nimo, what's going on? You were almost a minute slower than Monday.
Not sure, Coach. I'm sorry.
You OK, Mo? You look kind of tired.
I'm fine. I just don't understand why my times are slipping.
I had to do better.
So that evening at Mom's house . . .
I'm going for a run. Be back soon!
A run? But you just got back from practice an hour ago.
Does your father let you go on these extra runs?

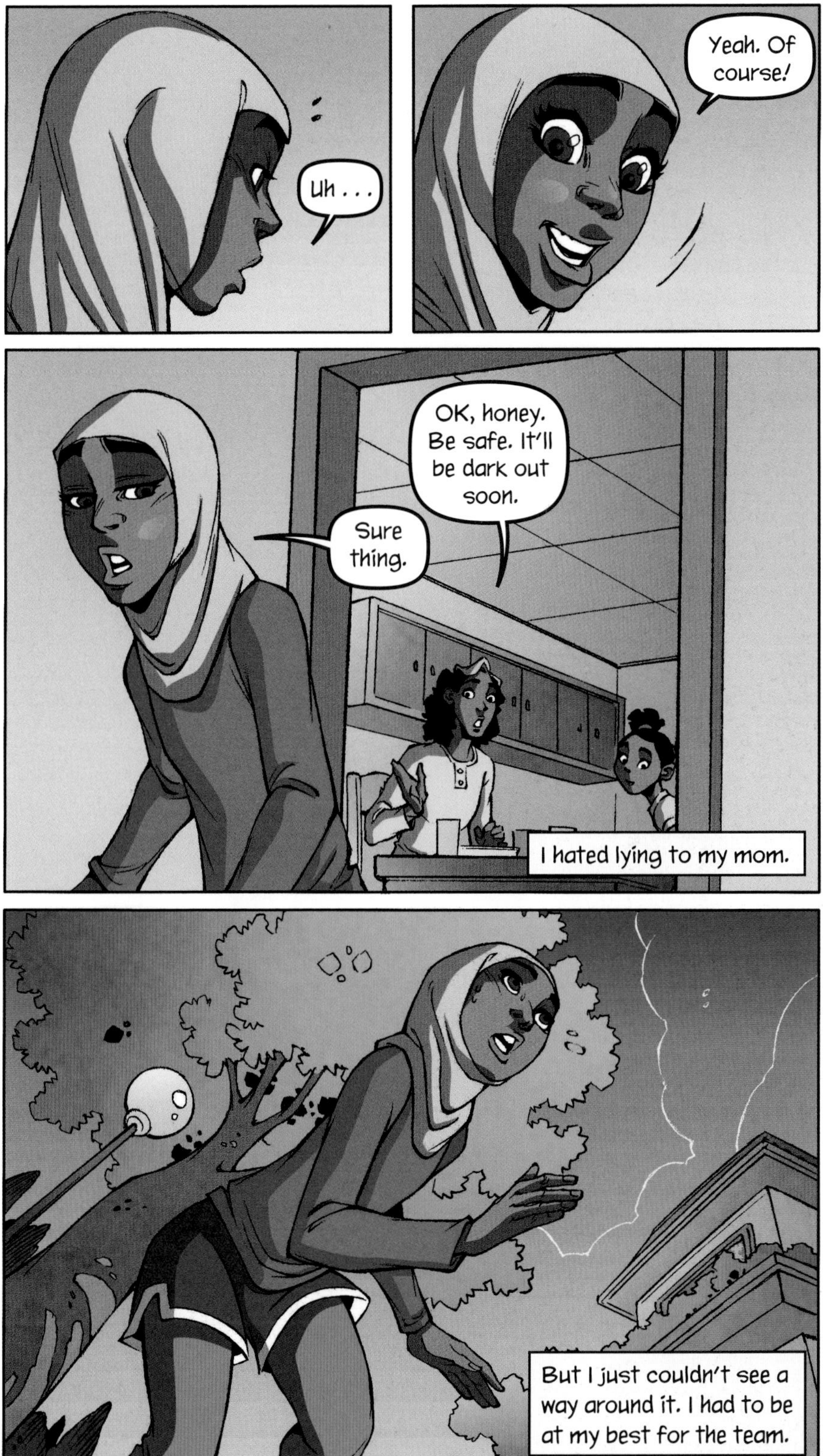
Uh . . .
Yeah. Of course!
OK, honey. Be safe. It'll be dark out soon.
Sure thing.
I hated lying to my mom.
But I just couldn't see a way around it. I had to be at my best for the team.

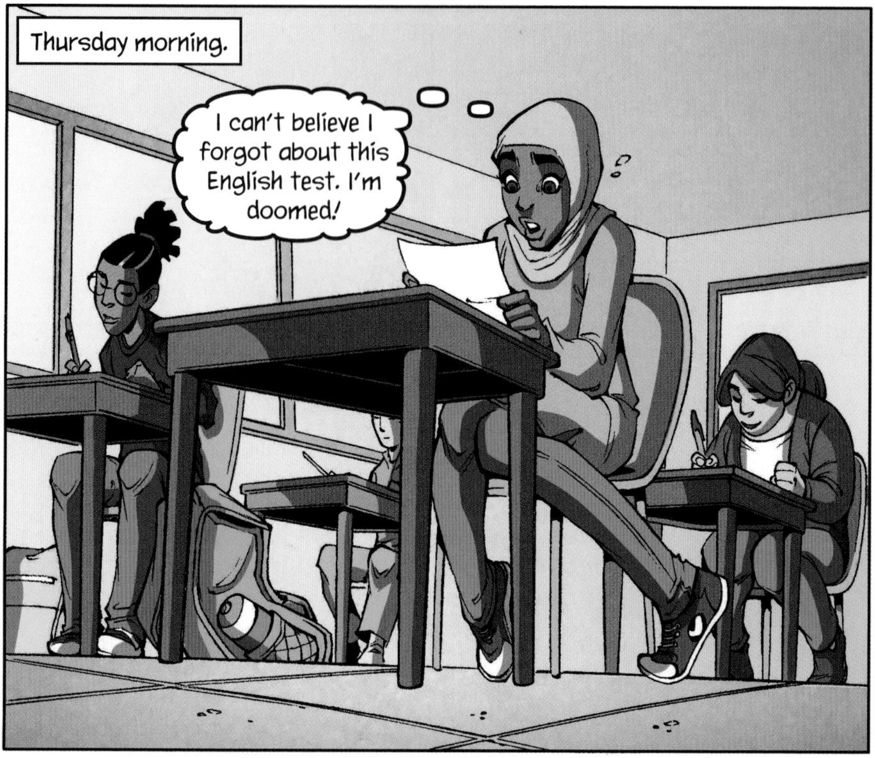
Thursday morning.
I can't believe I forgot about this English test. I'm doomed!

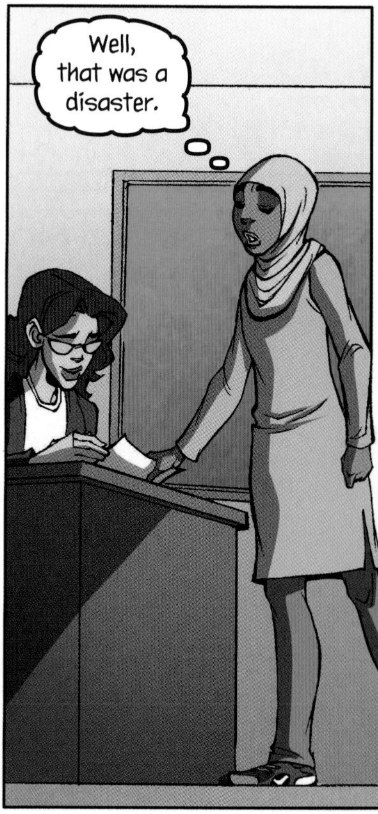
Well, that was a disaster.

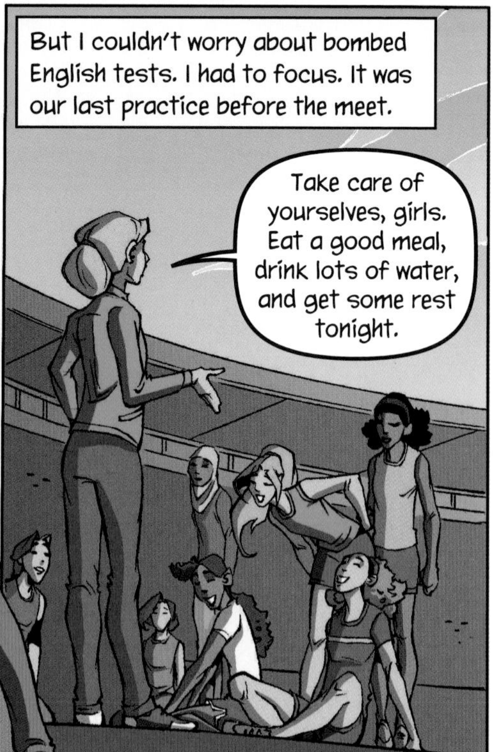
But I couldn't worry about bombed English tests. I had to focus. It was our last practice before the meet.
Take care of yourselves, girls. Eat a good meal, drink lots of water, and get some rest tonight.

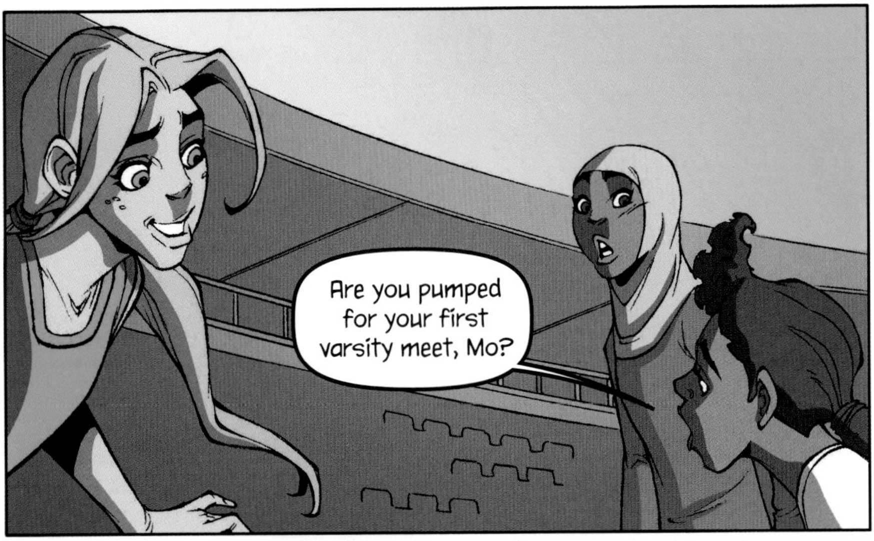
Are you pumped for your first varsity meet, Mo?

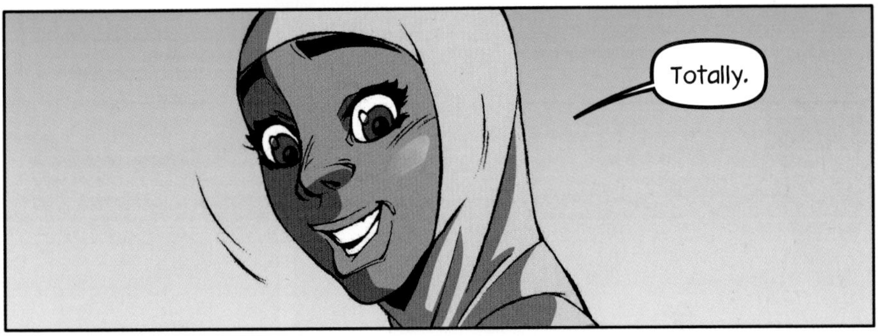
Totally.

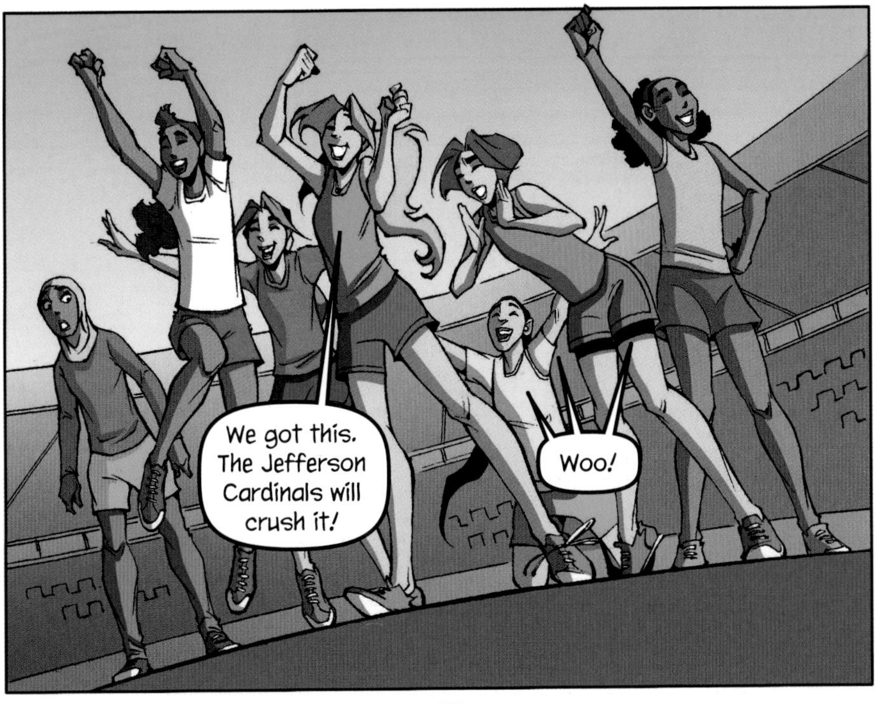
We got this. The Jefferson Cardinals will crush it!
Woo!

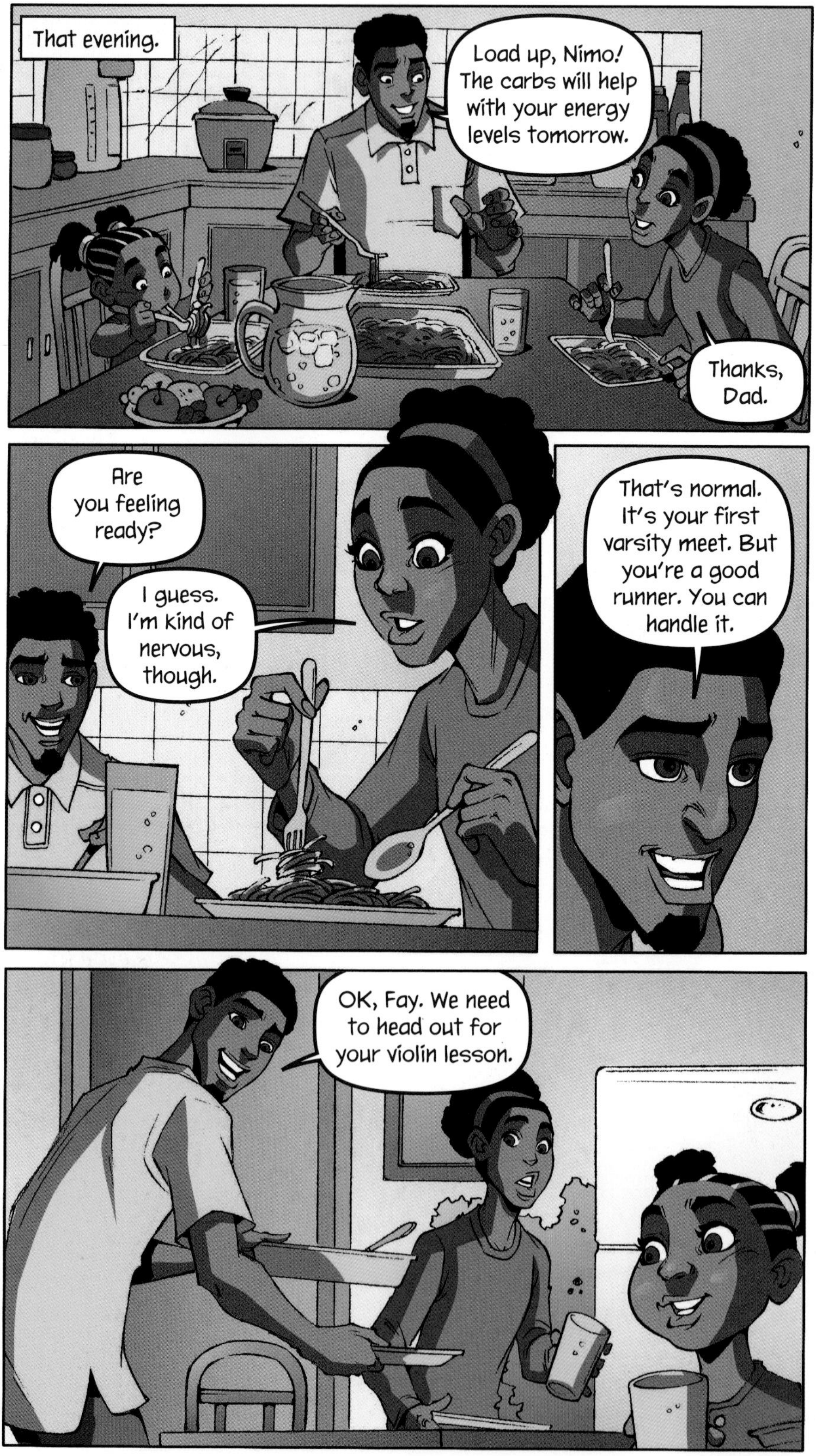
That evening.
Load up, Nimo! The carbs will help with your energy levels tomorrow.
Thanks, Dad.
Are you feeling ready?
I guess. I'm kind of nervous, though.
That's normal. It's your first varsity meet. But you're a good runner. You can handle it.
OK, Fay. We need to head out for your violin lesson.

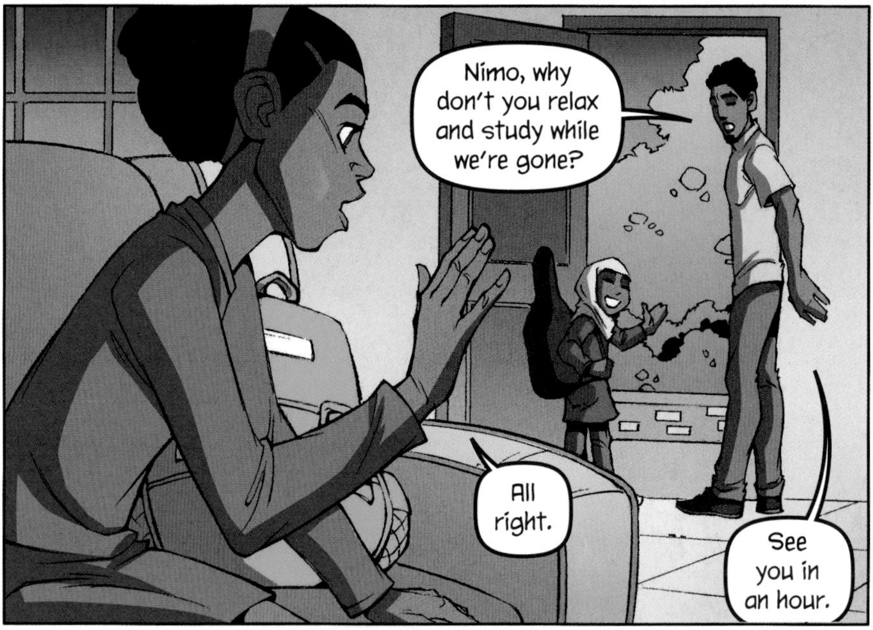
Nimo, why don't you relax and study while we're gone?
All right.
See you in an hour.

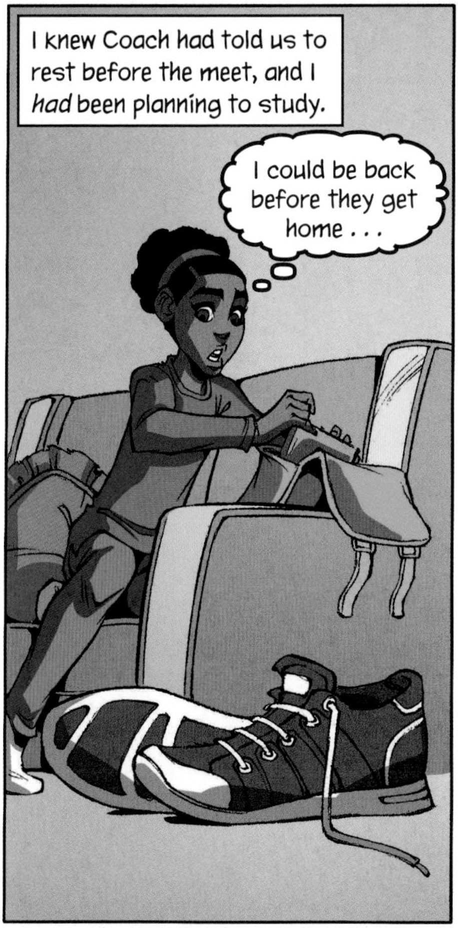
I knew Coach had told us to rest before the meet, and I *had* been planning to study.
I could be back before they get home . . .

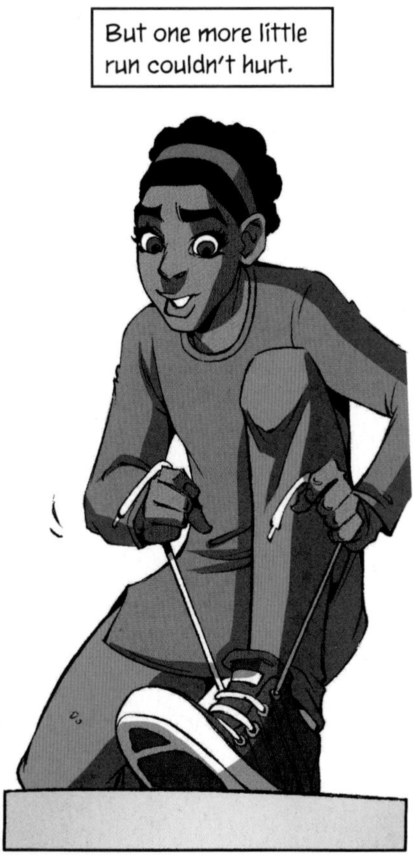
But one more little run couldn't hurt.

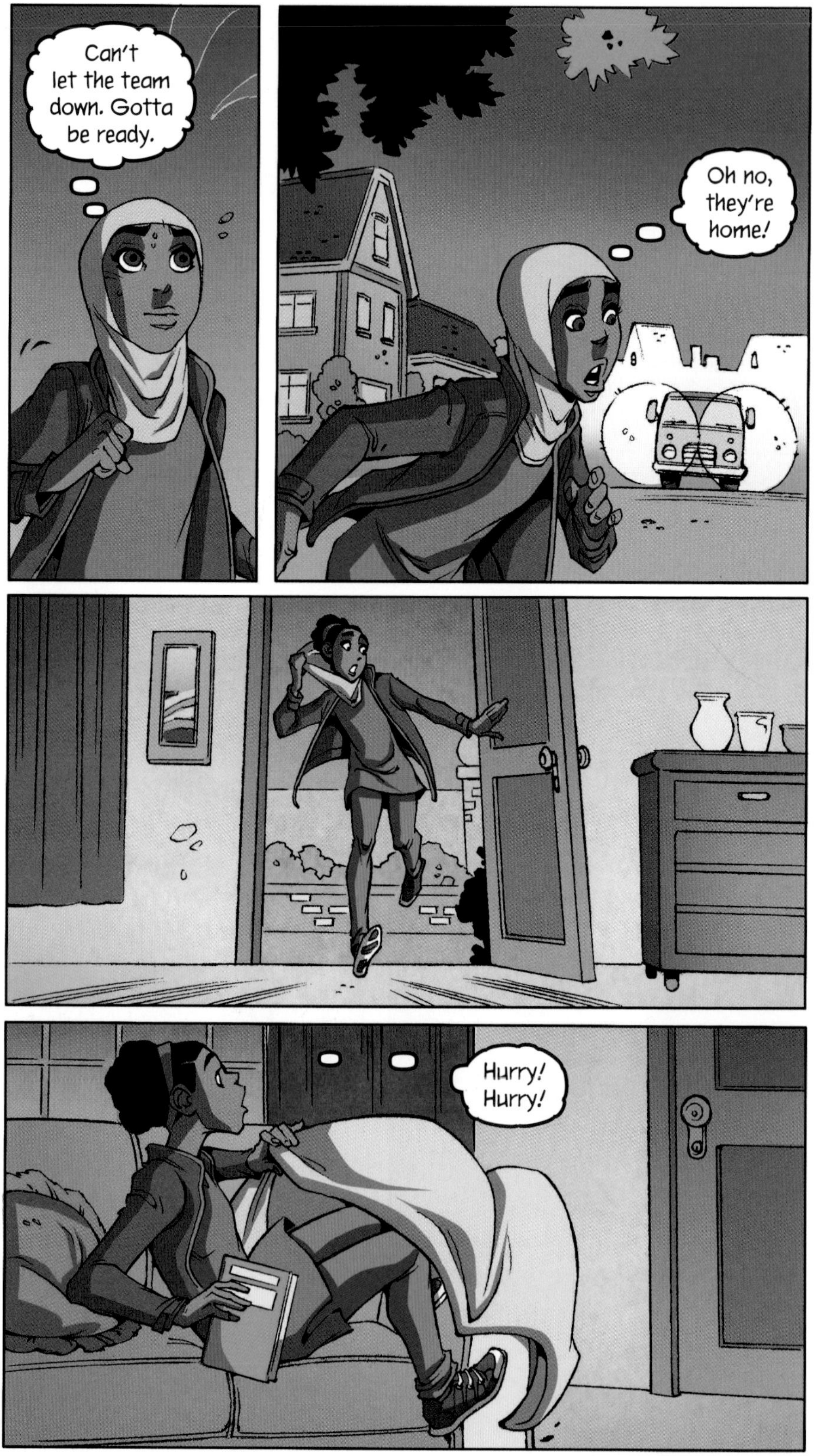
Can't let the team down. Gotta be ready.
Oh no, they're home!
Hurry! Hurry!

Hey, guys. How was your lesson, Fay?

It was OK.

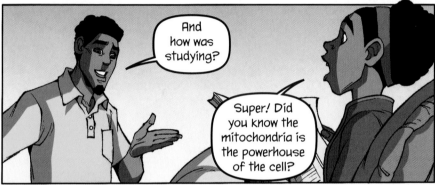

And how was studying?

Super! Did you know the mitochondria is the powerhouse of the cell?

Interesting. Well, you better get to bed. You have a big day tomorrow.

Good idea.

I just hoped I had done enough.

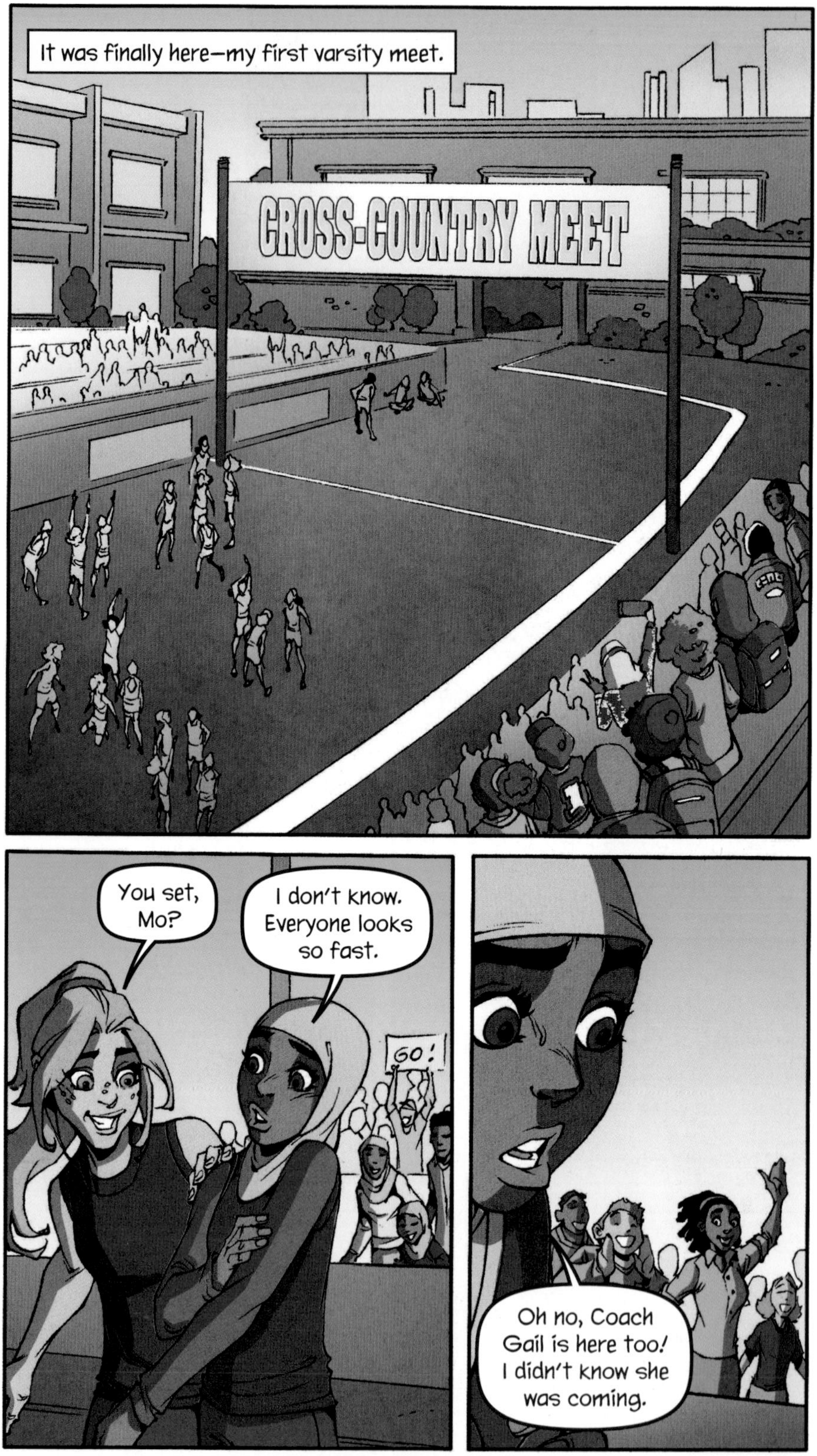
It was finally here—my first varsity meet.
CROSS-COUNTRY MEET
You set, Mo?
I don't know. Everyone looks so fast.
GO!
Oh no, Coach Gail is here too! I didn't know she was coming.

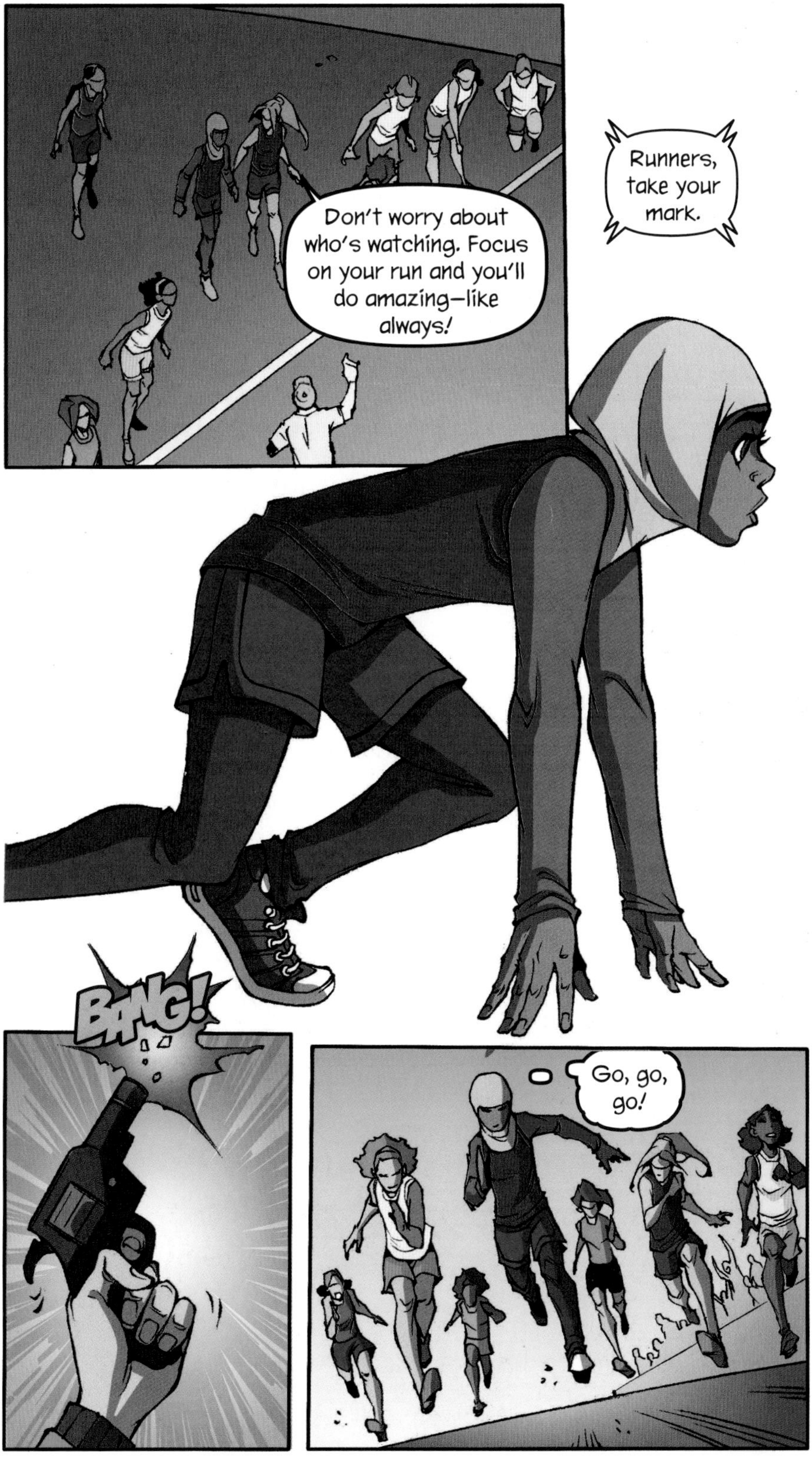
Don't worry about who's watching. Focus on your run and you'll do amazing—like always!
Runners, take your mark.
BANG!
Go, go, go!

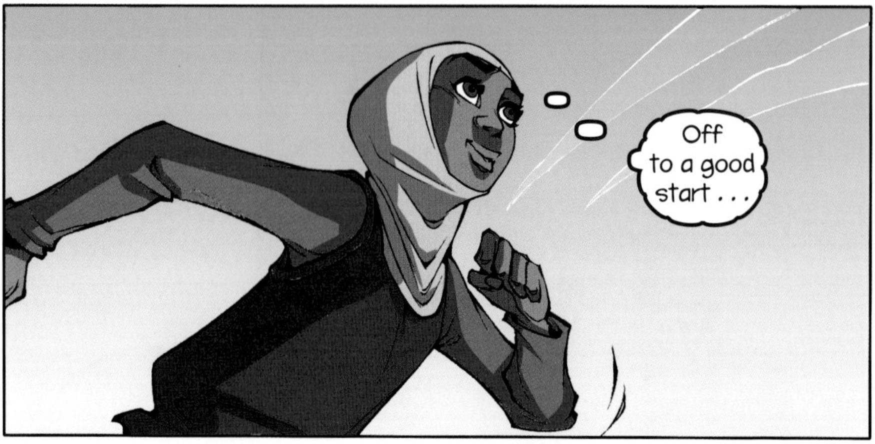
Off to a good start . . .

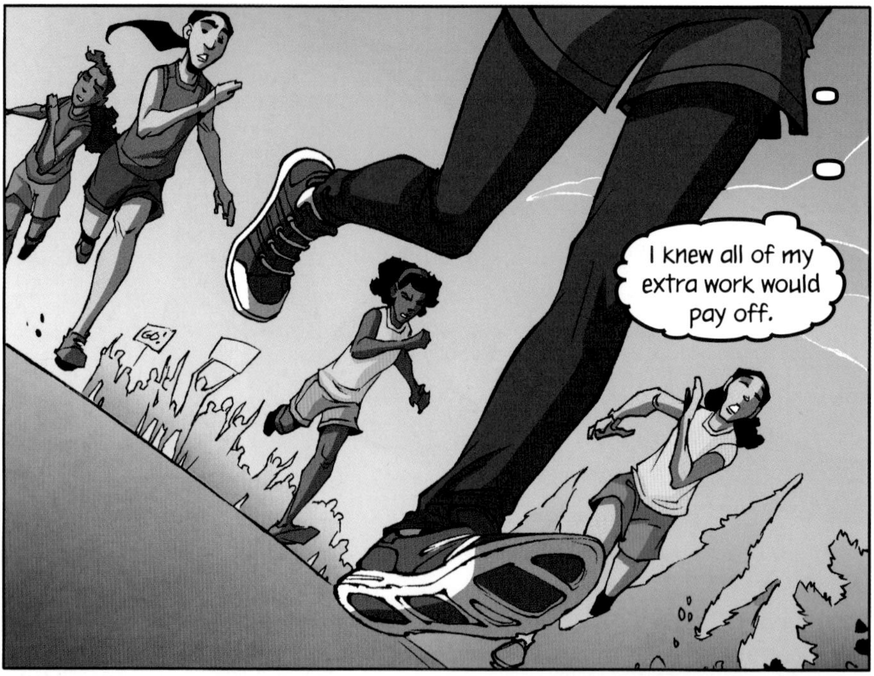
GO!
I knew all of my extra work would pay off.

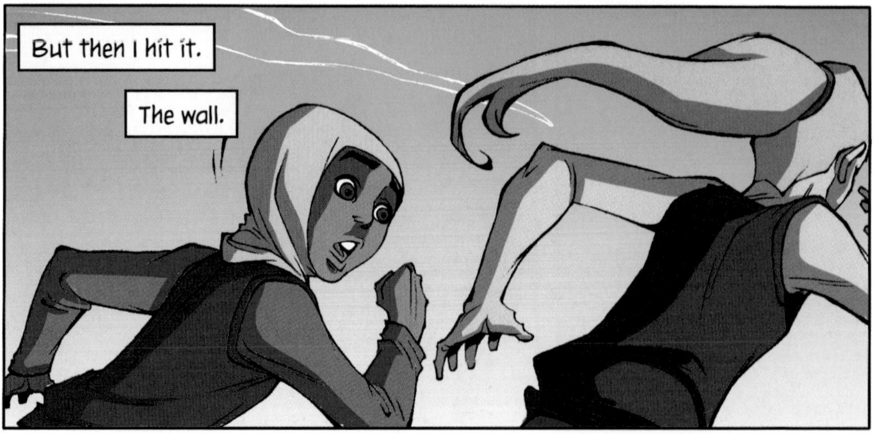
But then I hit it.
The wall.

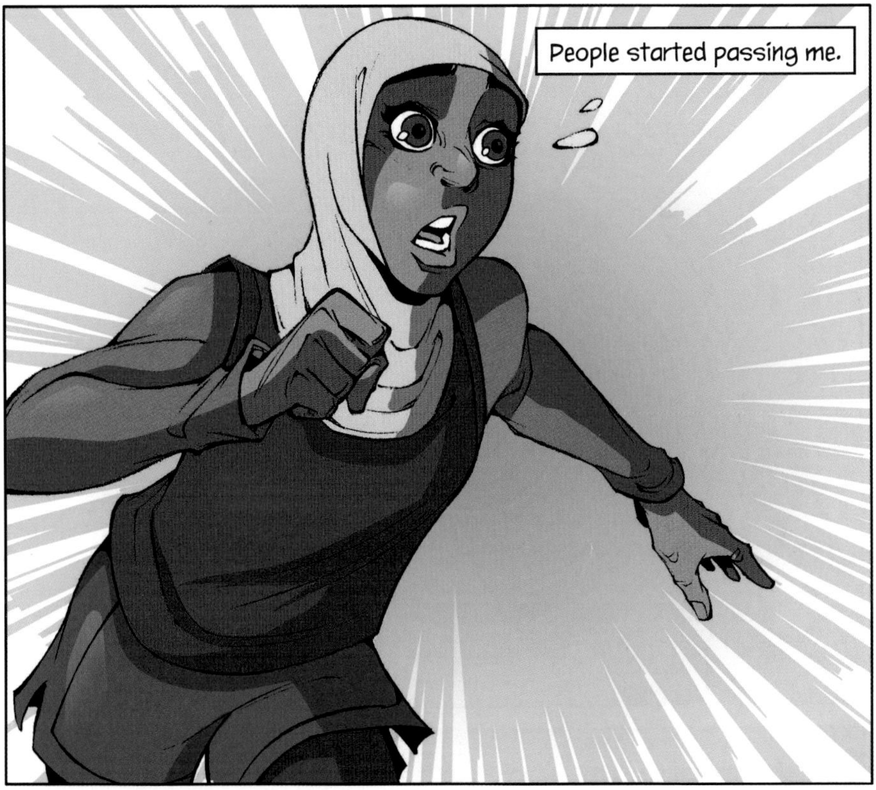
People started passing me.

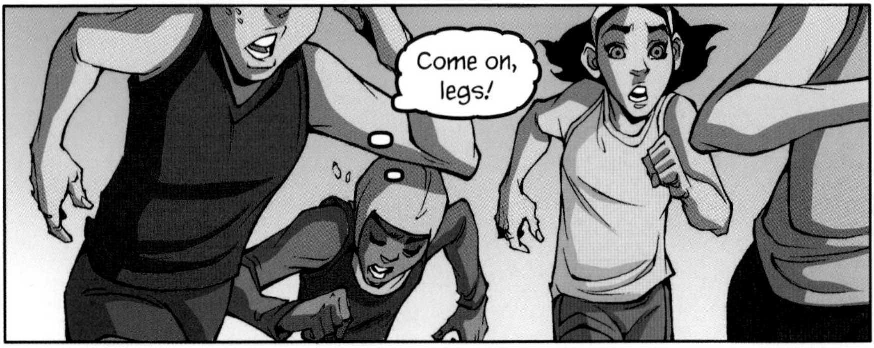
Come on, legs!

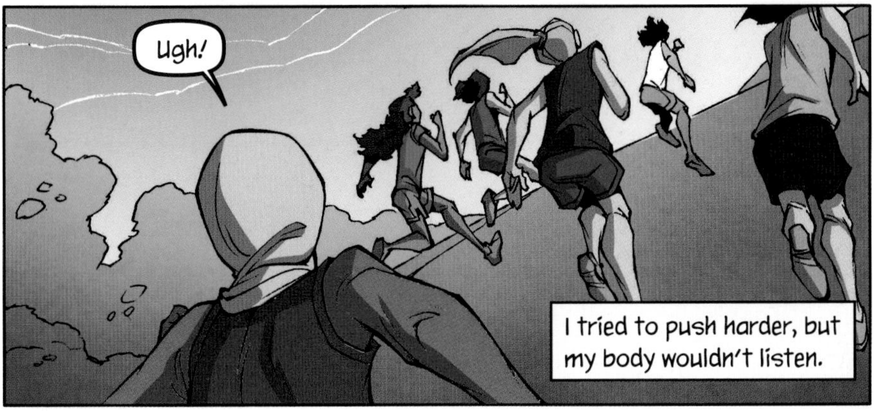
Ugh!
I tried to push harder, but my body wouldn't listen.

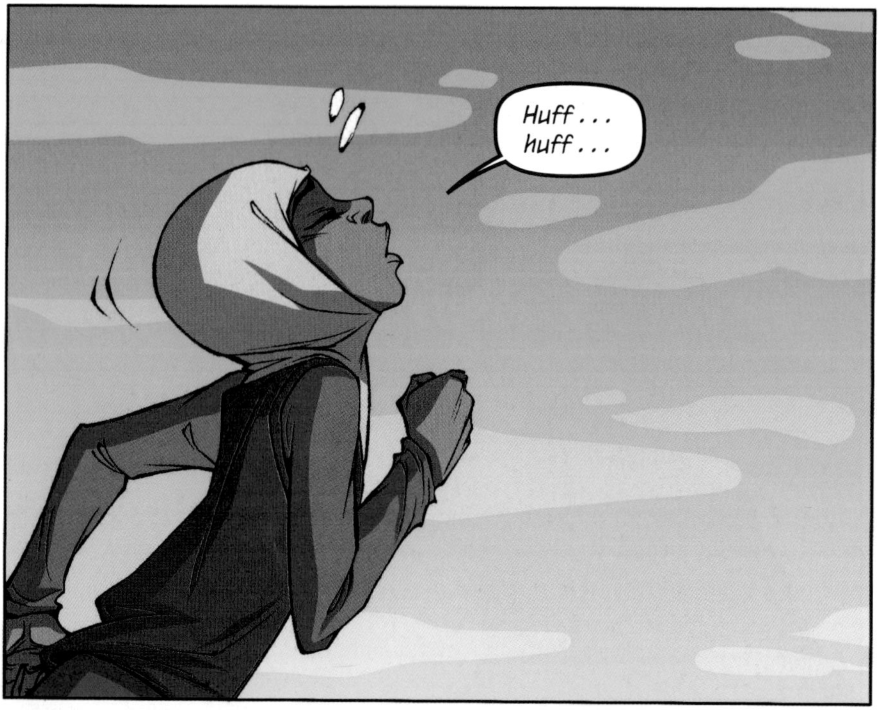
Huff . . .
huff . . .

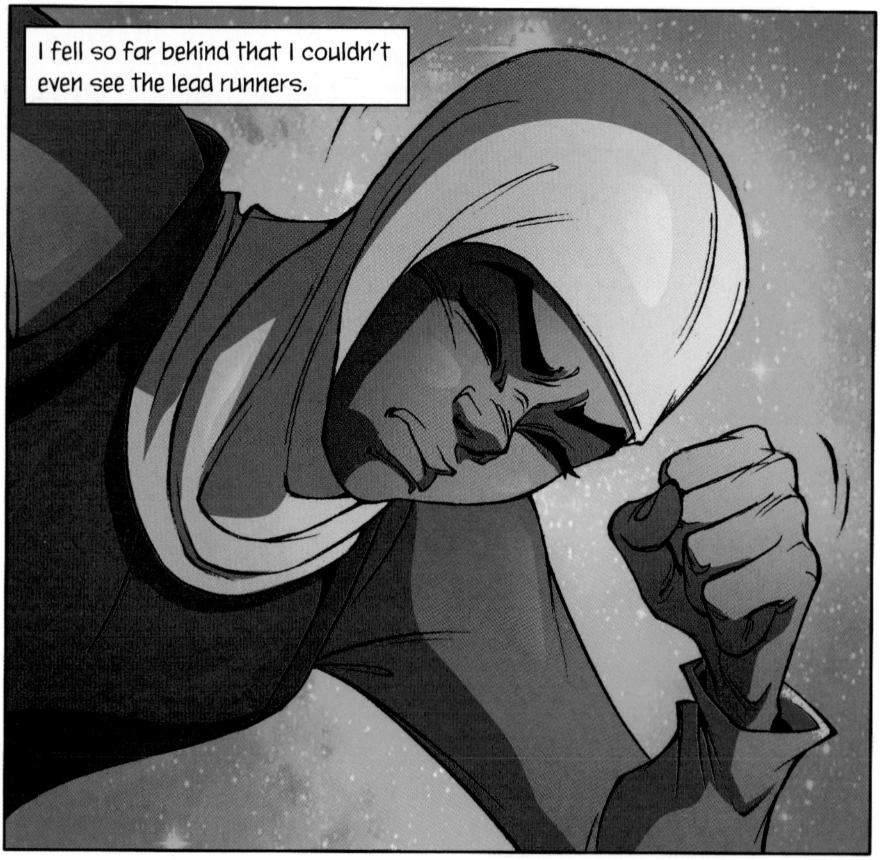
I fell so far behind that I couldn't even see the lead runners.

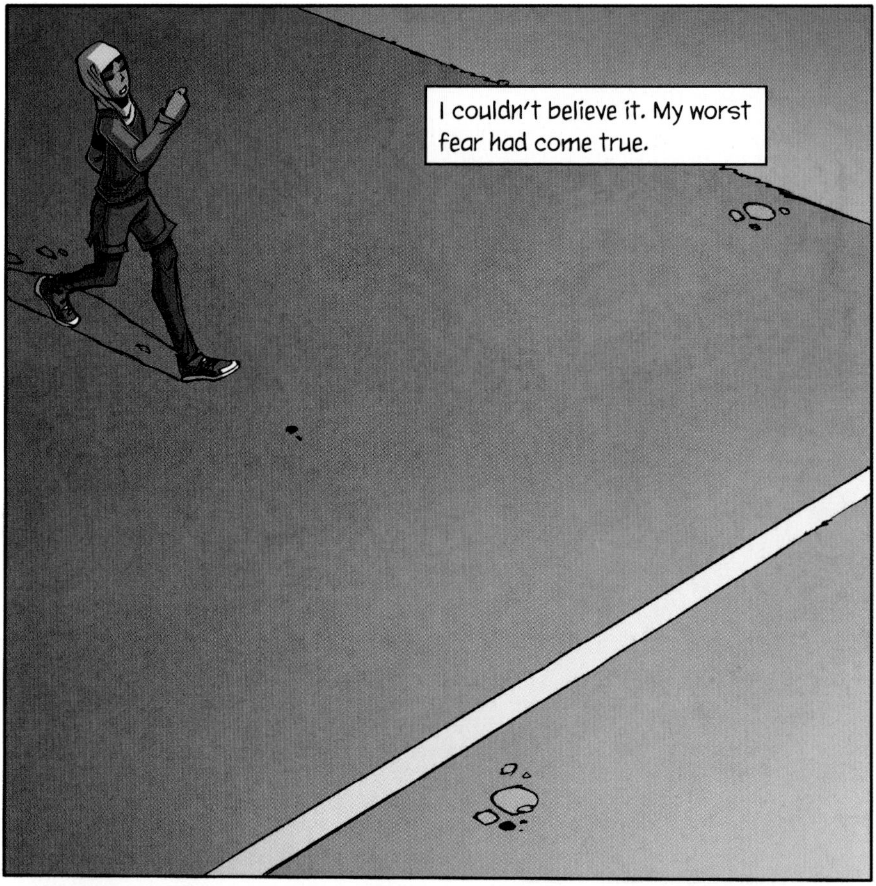
I couldn't believe it. My worst fear had come true.

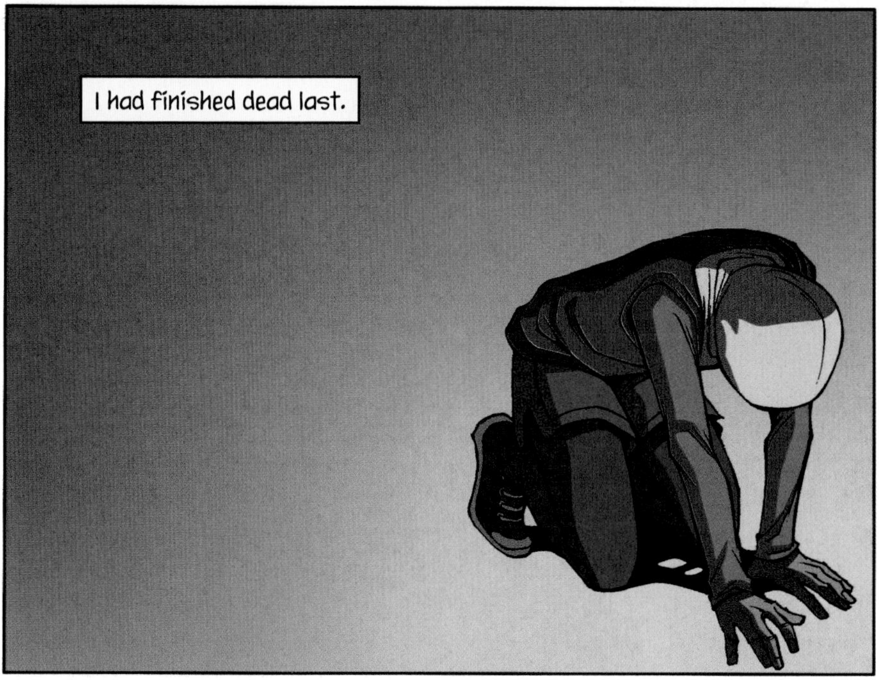
I had finished dead last.

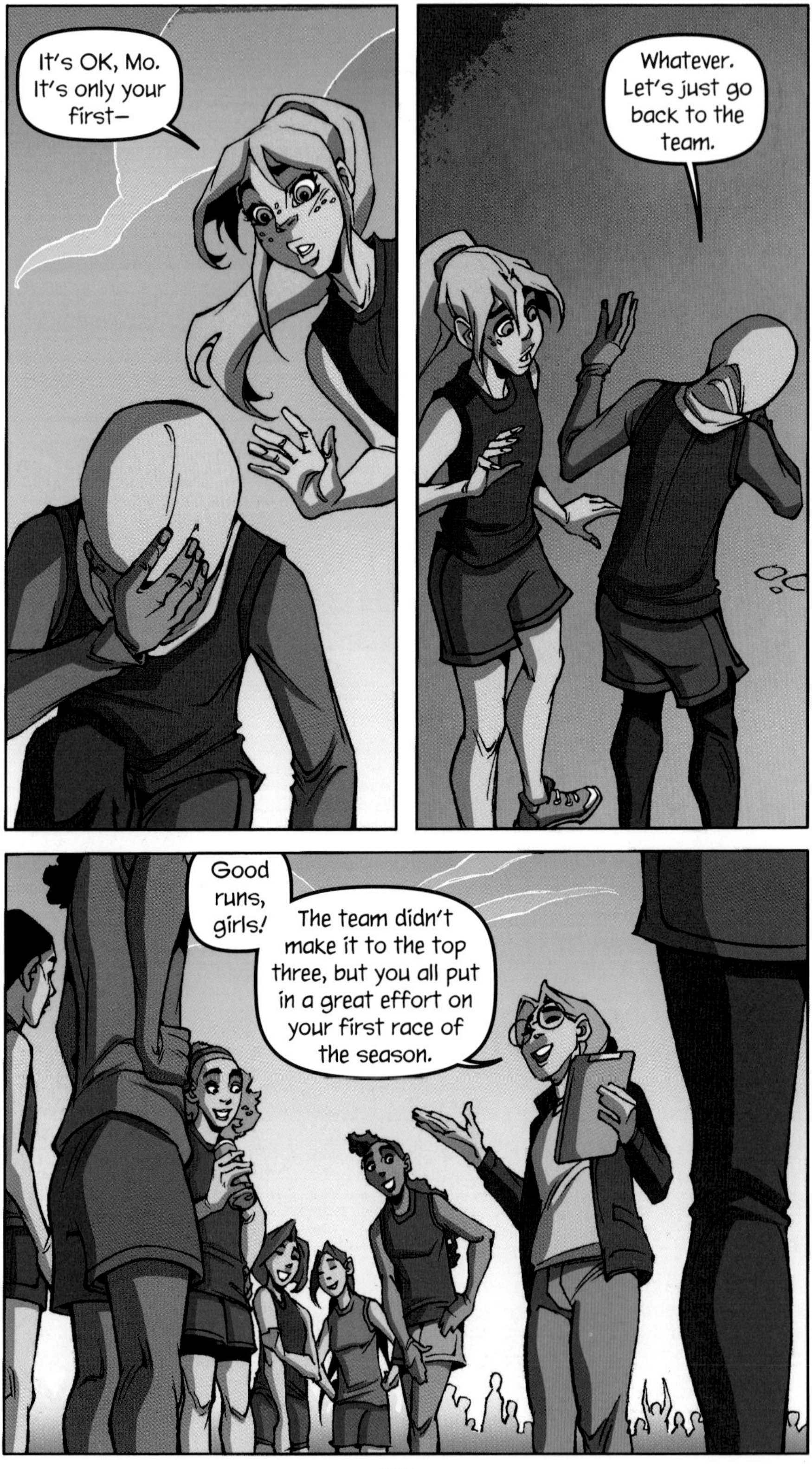
It's OK, Mo. It's only your first–
Whatever. Let's just go back to the team.
Good runs, girls!
The team didn't make it to the top three, but you all put in a great effort on your first race of the season.

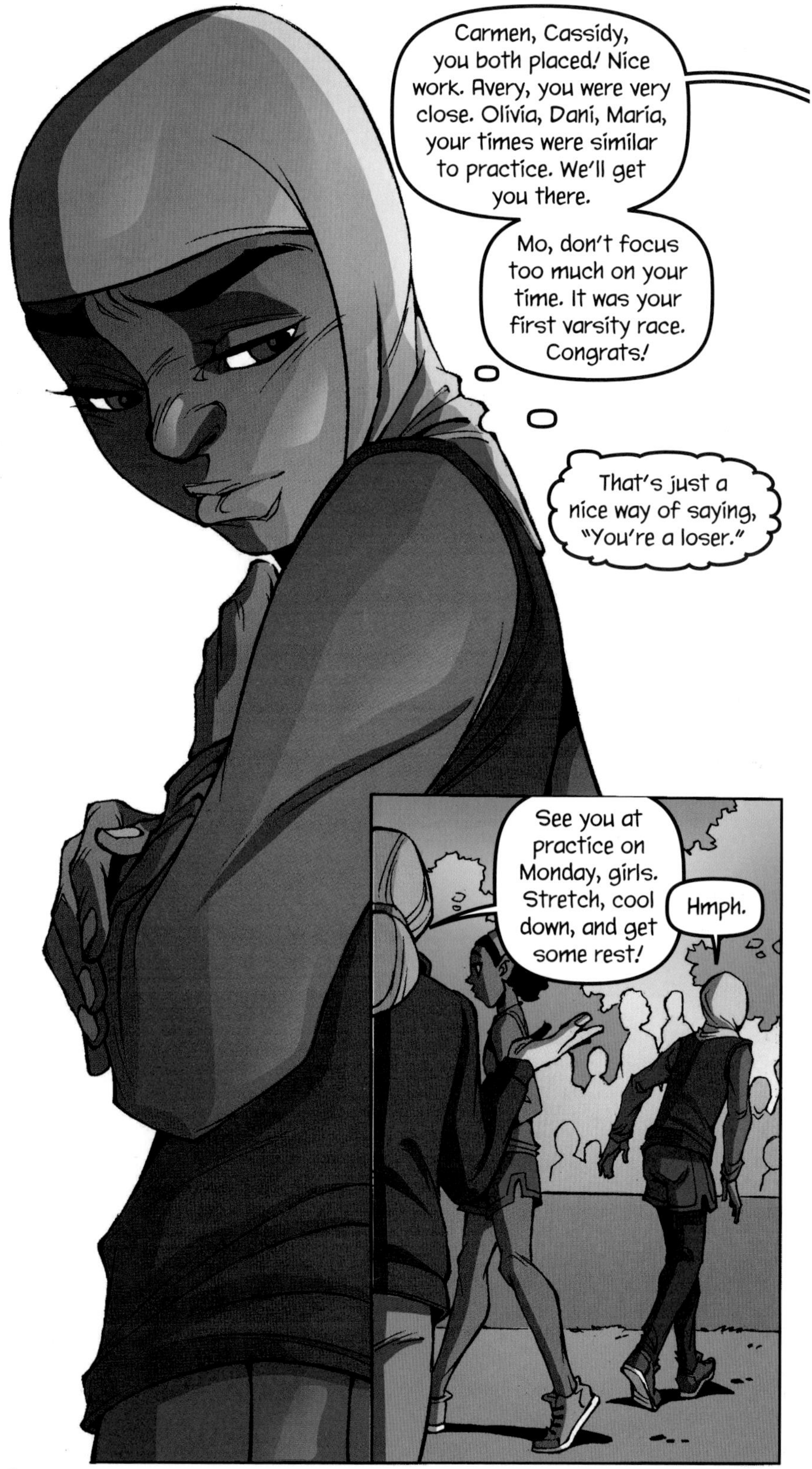
Carmen, Cassidy, you both placed! Nice work. Avery, you were very close. Olivia, Dani, Maria, your times were similar to practice. We'll get you there.
Mo, don't focus too much on your time. It was your first varsity race. Congrats!
That's just a nice way of saying, "You're a loser."
See you at practice on Monday, girls. Stretch, cool down, and get some rest!
Hmph.

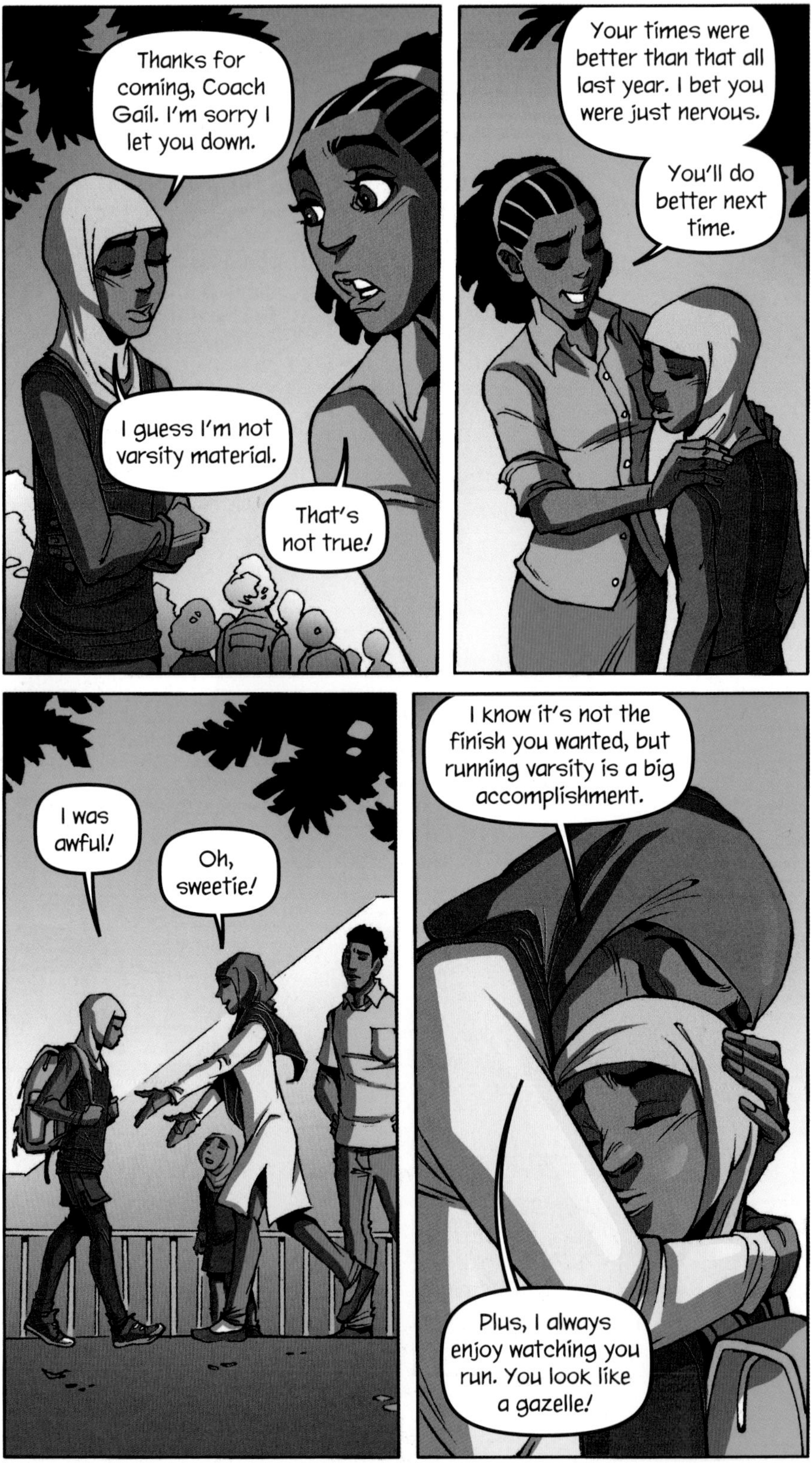

Thanks for coming, Coach Gail. I'm sorry I let you down.
I guess I'm not varsity material.
That's not true!
Your times were better than that all last year. I bet you were just nervous.
You'll do better next time.
I was awful!
Oh, sweetie!
I know it's not the finish you wanted, but running varsity is a big accomplishment.
Plus, I always enjoy watching you run. You look like a gazelle!

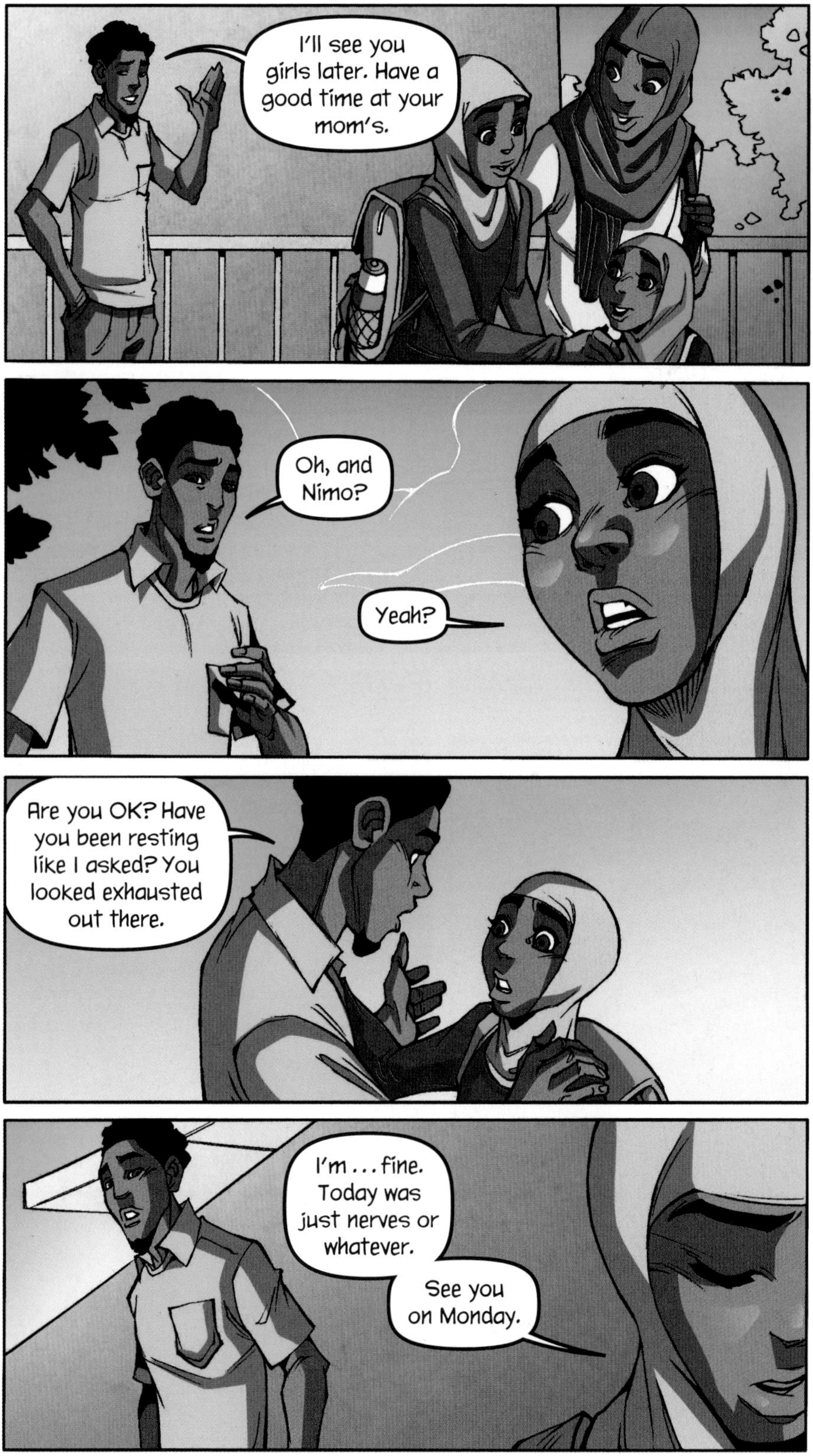
I'll see you girls later. Have a good time at your mom's.
Oh, and Nimo?
Yeah?
Are you OK? Have you been resting like I asked? You looked exhausted out there.
I'm . . . fine. Today was just nerves or whatever.
See you on Monday.

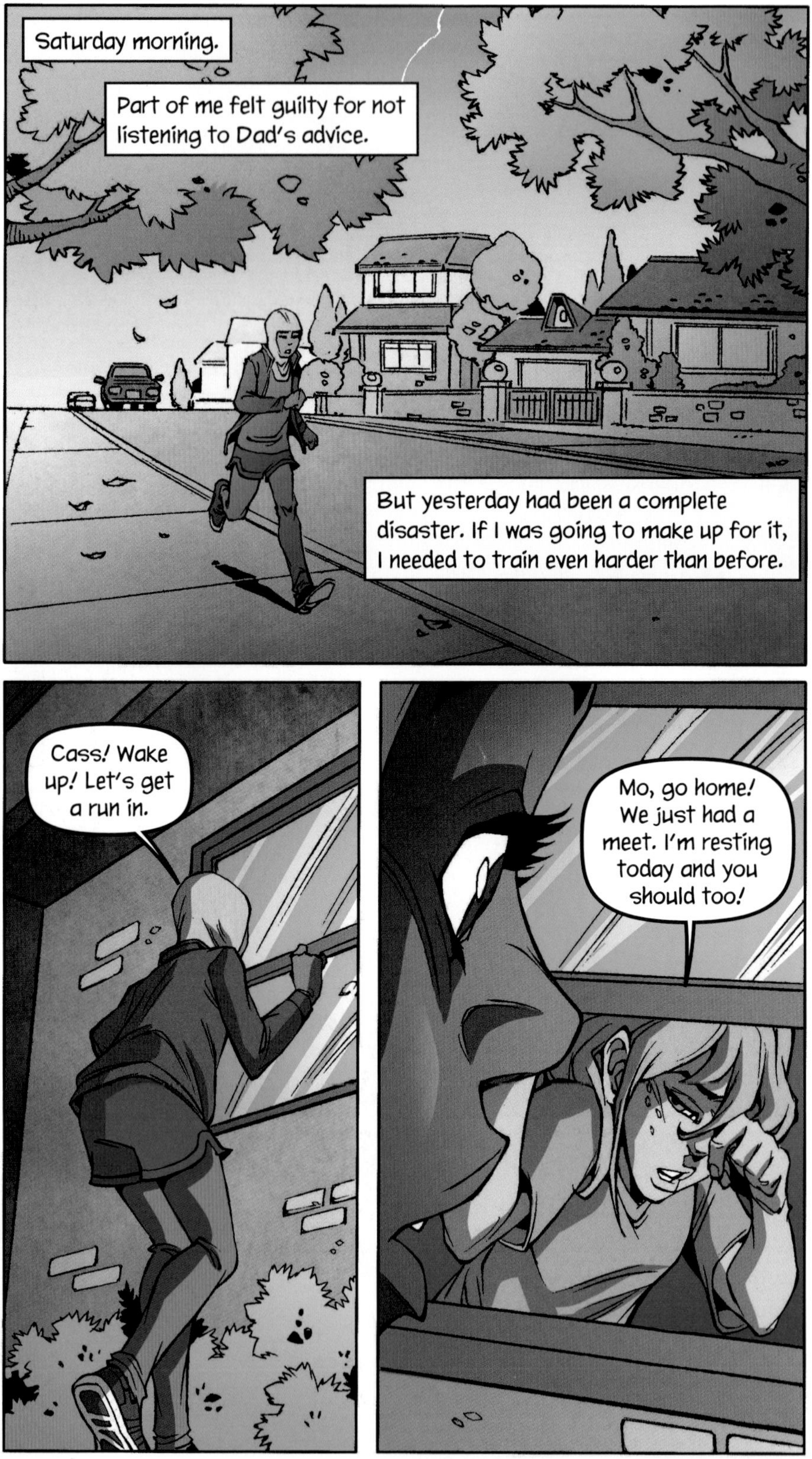
Saturday morning.
Part of me felt guilty for not listening to Dad's advice.
But yesterday had been a complete disaster. If I was going to make up for it, I needed to train even harder than before.
Cass! Wake up! Let's get a run in.
Mo, go home! We just had a meet. I'm resting today and you should too!

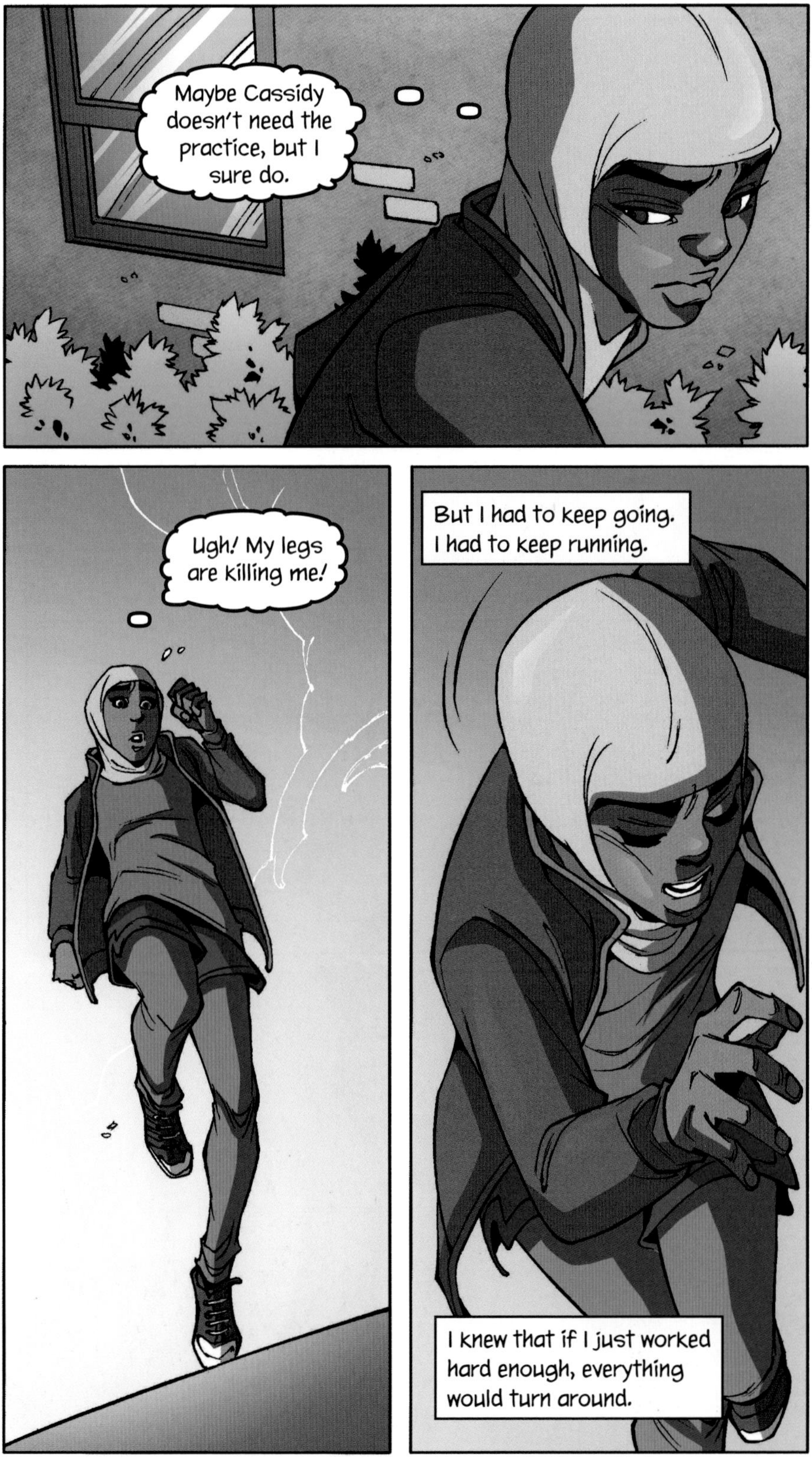
Maybe Cassidy doesn't need the practice, but I sure do.
Ugh! My legs are killing me!
But I had to keep going. I had to keep running.
I knew that if I just worked hard enough, everything would turn around.

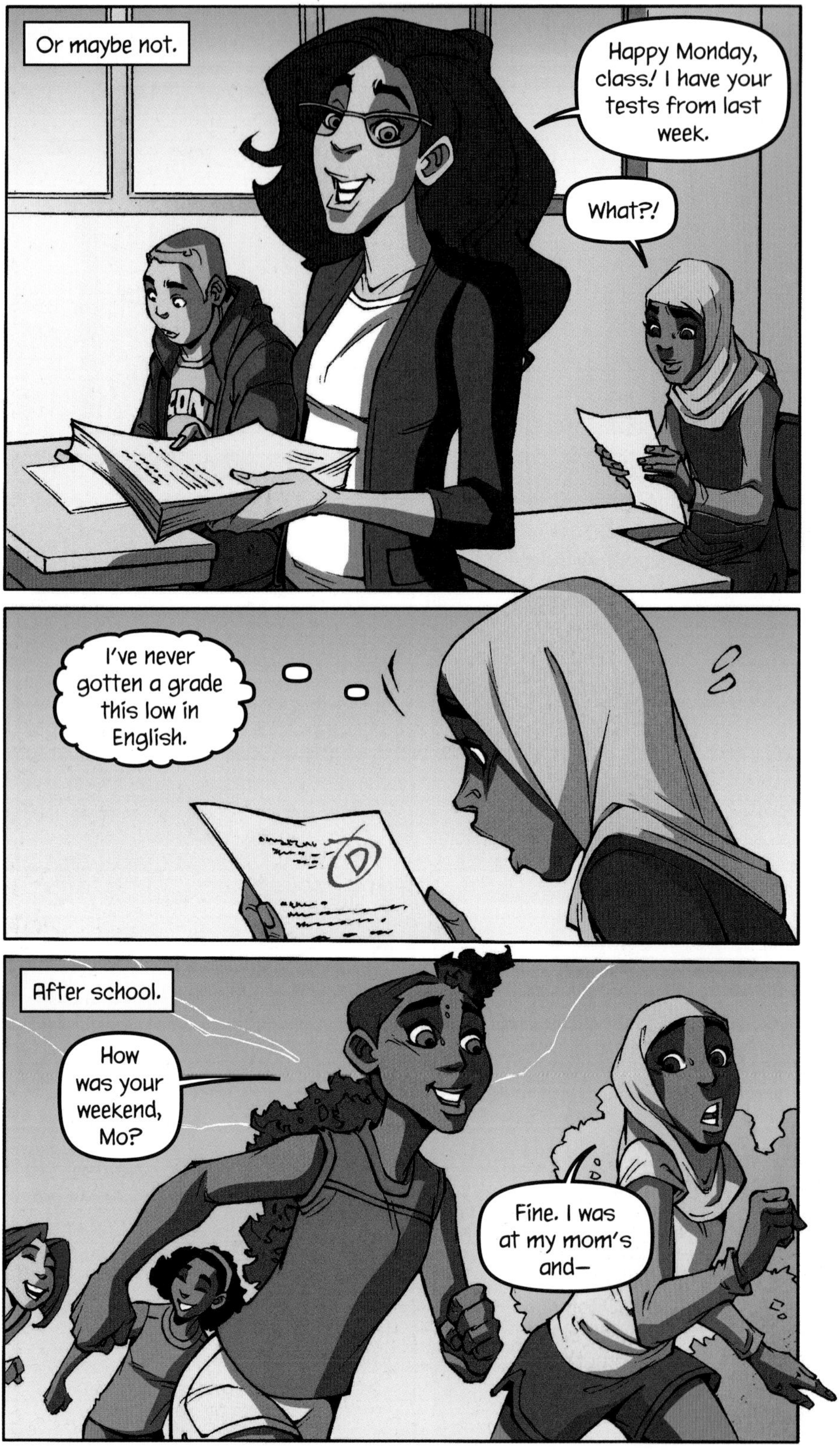
Or maybe not.
Happy Monday, class! I have your tests from last week.
What?!
I've never gotten a grade this low in English.
After school.
How was your weekend, Mo?
Fine. I was at my mom's and—

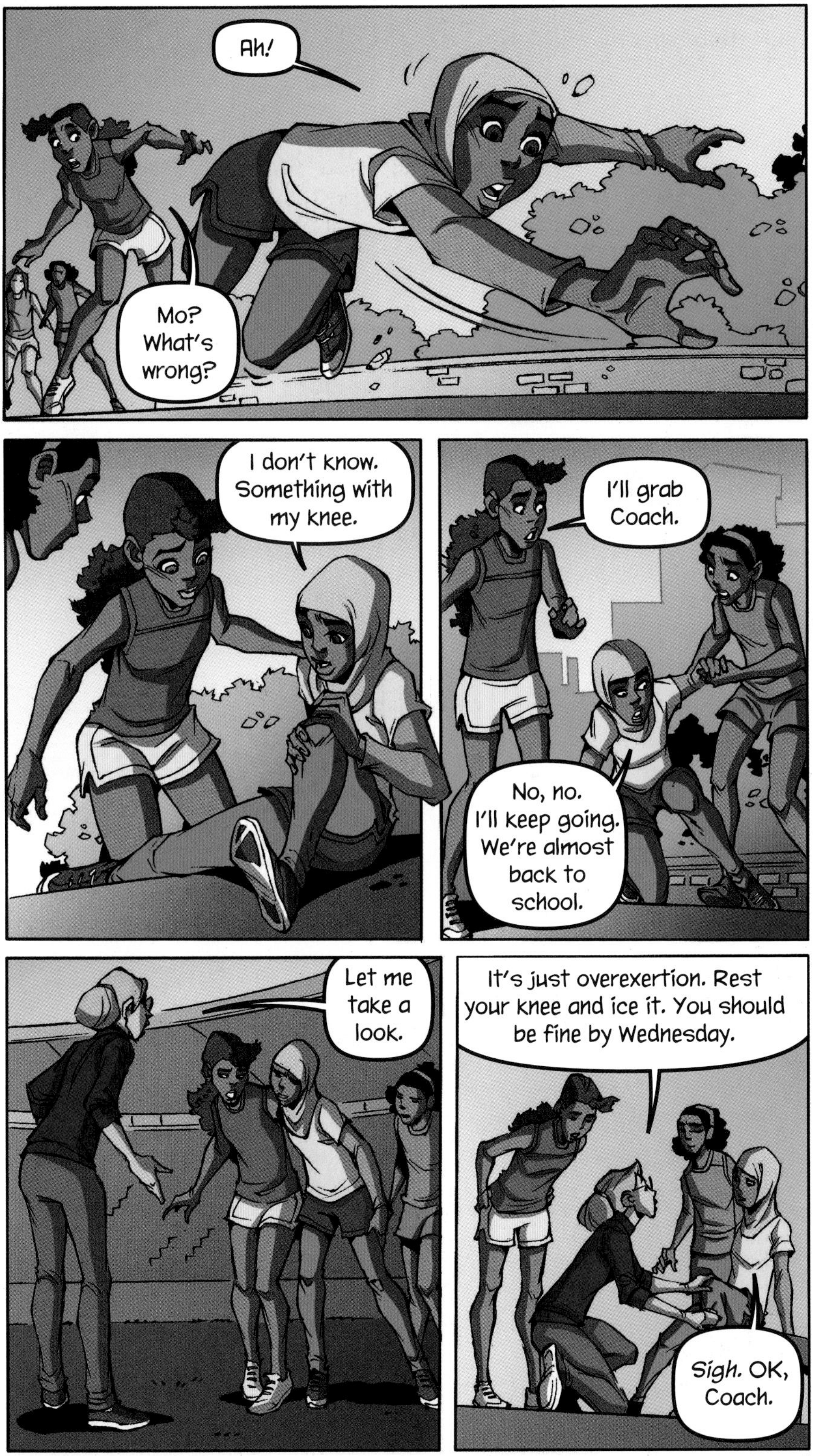
Ah!
Mo? What's wrong?
I don't know. Something with my knee.
I'll grab Coach.
No, no. I'll keep going. We're almost back to school.
Let me take a look.
It's just overexertion. Rest your knee and ice it. You should be fine by Wednesday.
Sigh. OK, Coach.

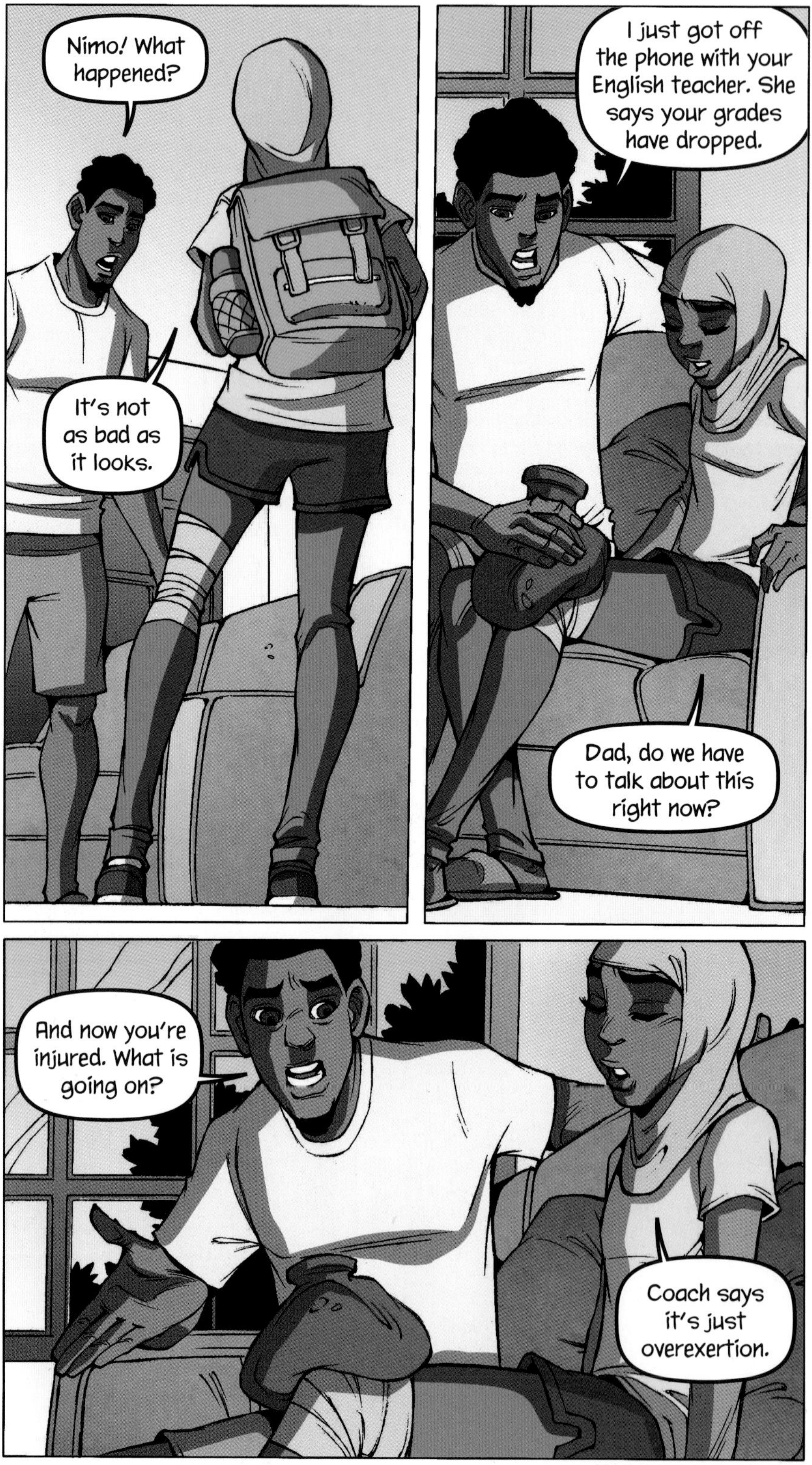
Nimo! What happened?
It's not as bad as it looks.
I just got off the phone with your English teacher. She says your grades have dropped.
Dad, do we have to talk about this right now?
And now you're injured. What is going on?
Coach says it's just overexertion.

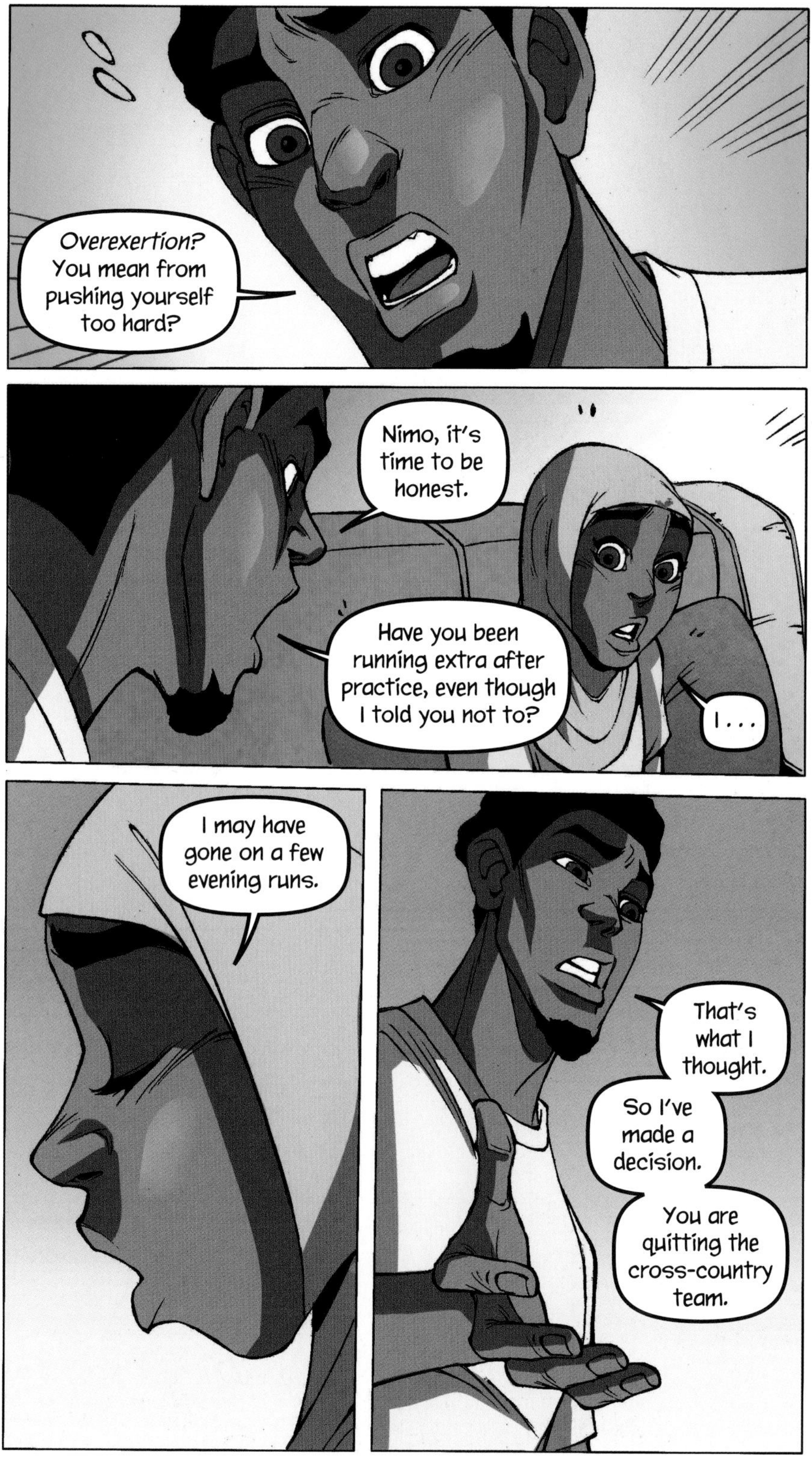
Overexertion? You mean from pushing yourself too hard?
Nimo, it's time to be honest.
Have you been running extra after practice, even though I told you not to?
I . . .
I may have gone on a few evening runs.
That's what I thought.
So I've made a decision.
You are quitting the cross-country team.

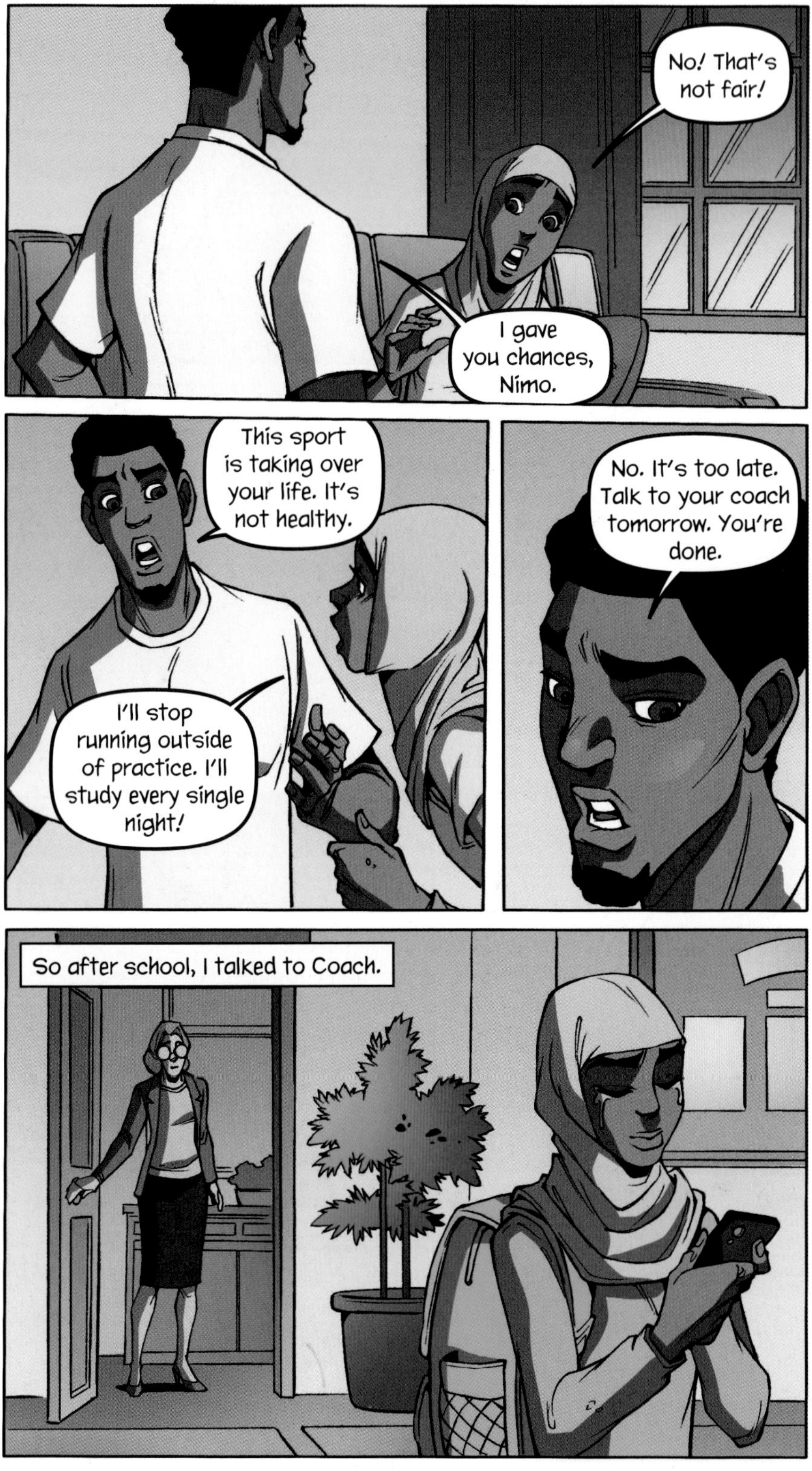
No! That's not fair!
I gave you chances, Nimo.
This sport is taking over your life. It's not healthy.
I'll stop running outside of practice. I'll study every single night!
No. It's too late. Talk to your coach tomorrow. You're done.
So after school, I talked to Coach.

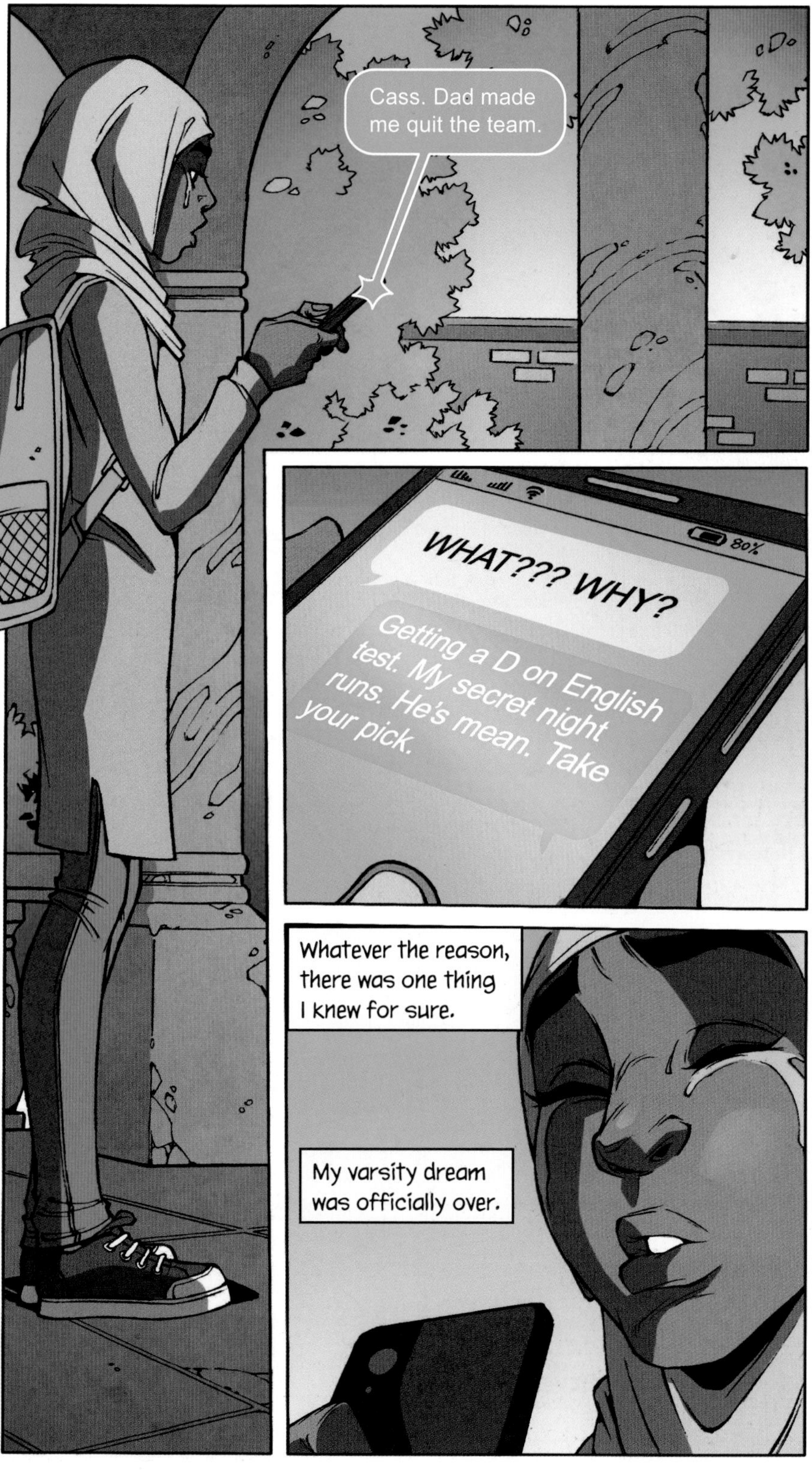
Cass. Dad made me quit the team.
80%
WHAT??? WHY?
Getting a D on English test. My secret night runs. He's mean. Take your pick.
Whatever the reason, there was one thing I knew for sure.
My varsity dream was officially over.

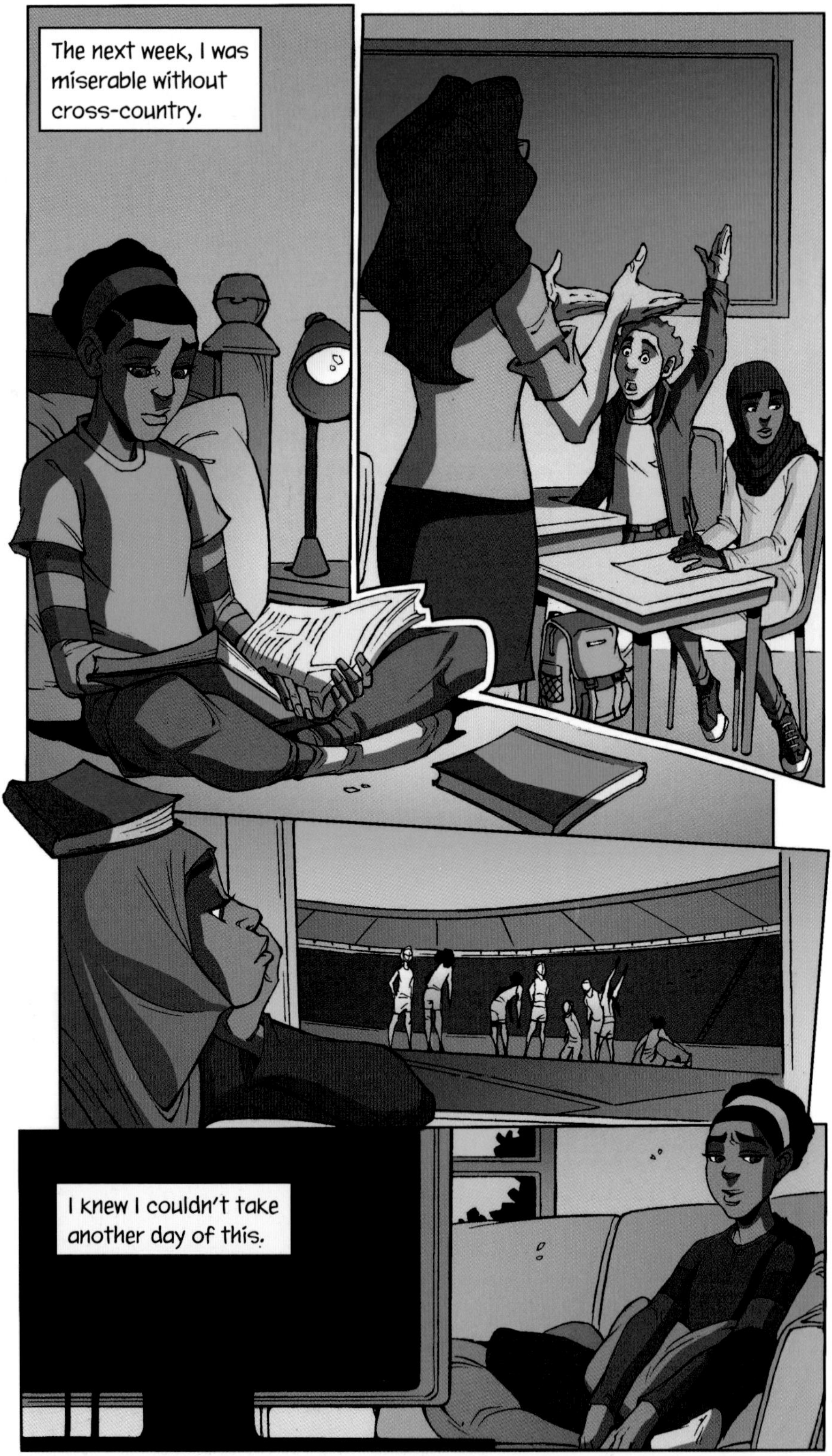
The next week, I was miserable without cross-country.
I knew I couldn't take another day of this.

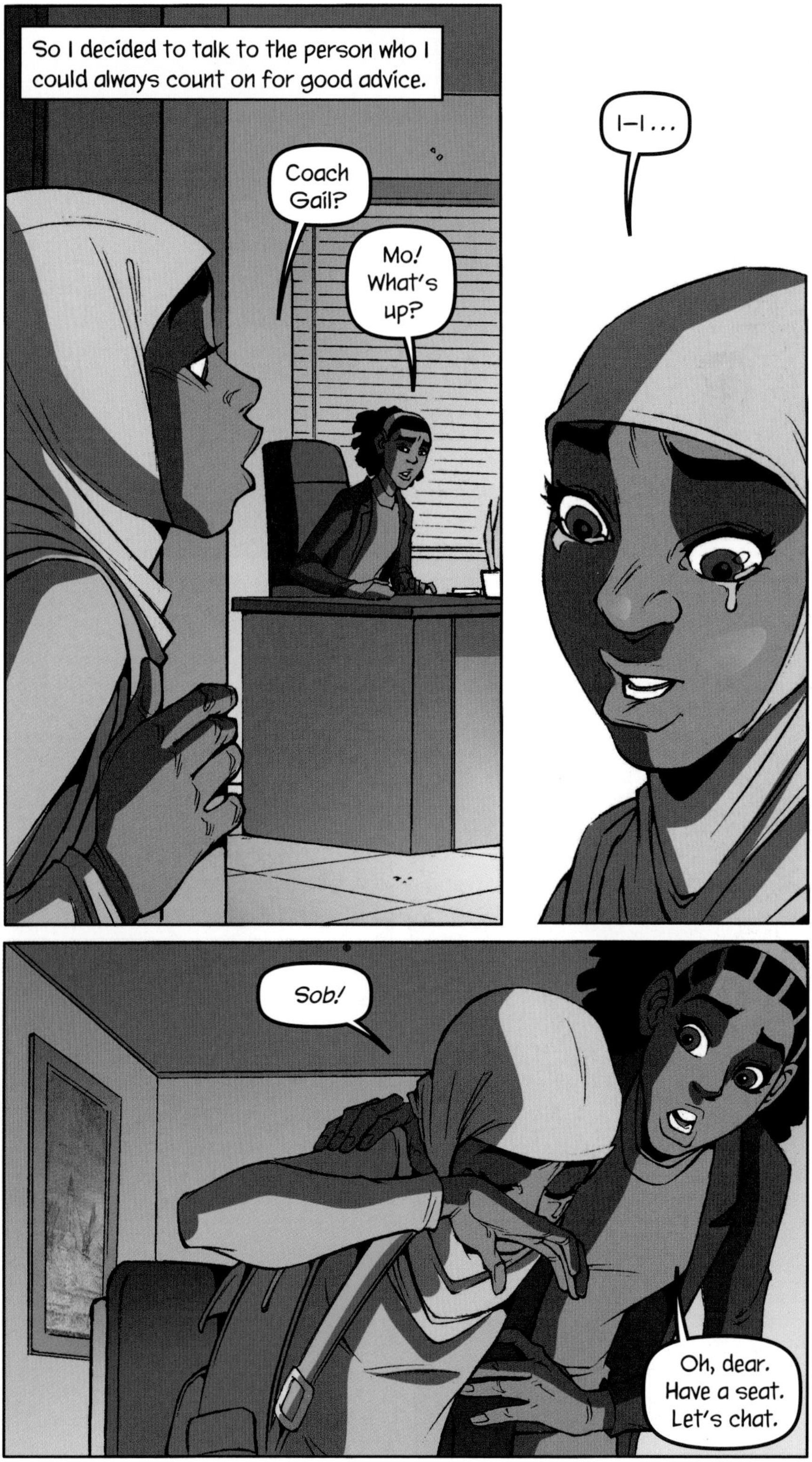
So I decided to talk to the person who I could always count on for good advice.
Coach Gail?
Mo! What's up?
I–I . . .
Sob!
Oh, dear. Have a seat. Let's chat.

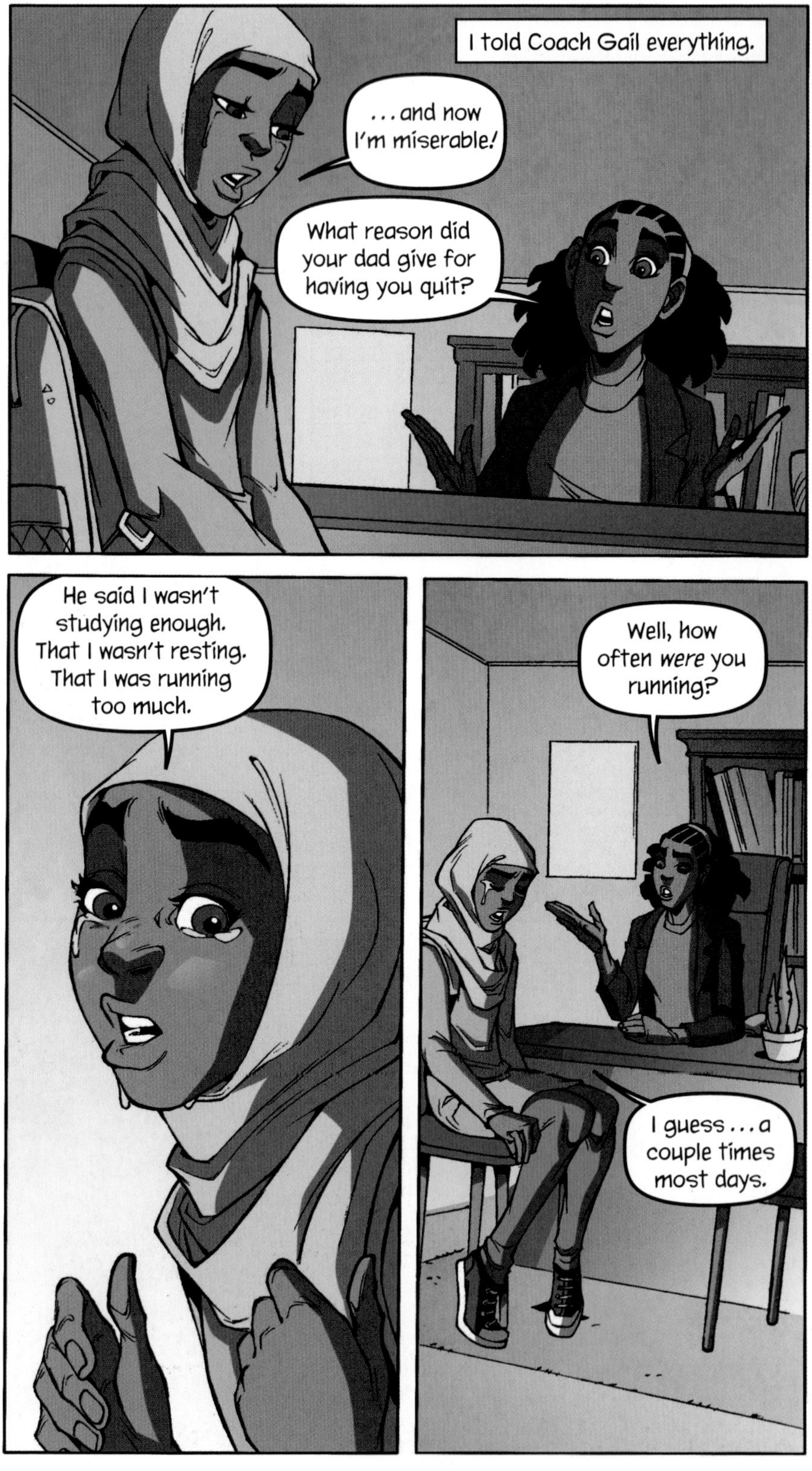
I told Coach Gail everything.
. . . and now I'm miserable!
What reason did your dad give for having you quit?
He said I wasn't studying enough. That I wasn't resting. That I was running too much.
Well, how often *were* you running?
I guess . . . a couple times most days.

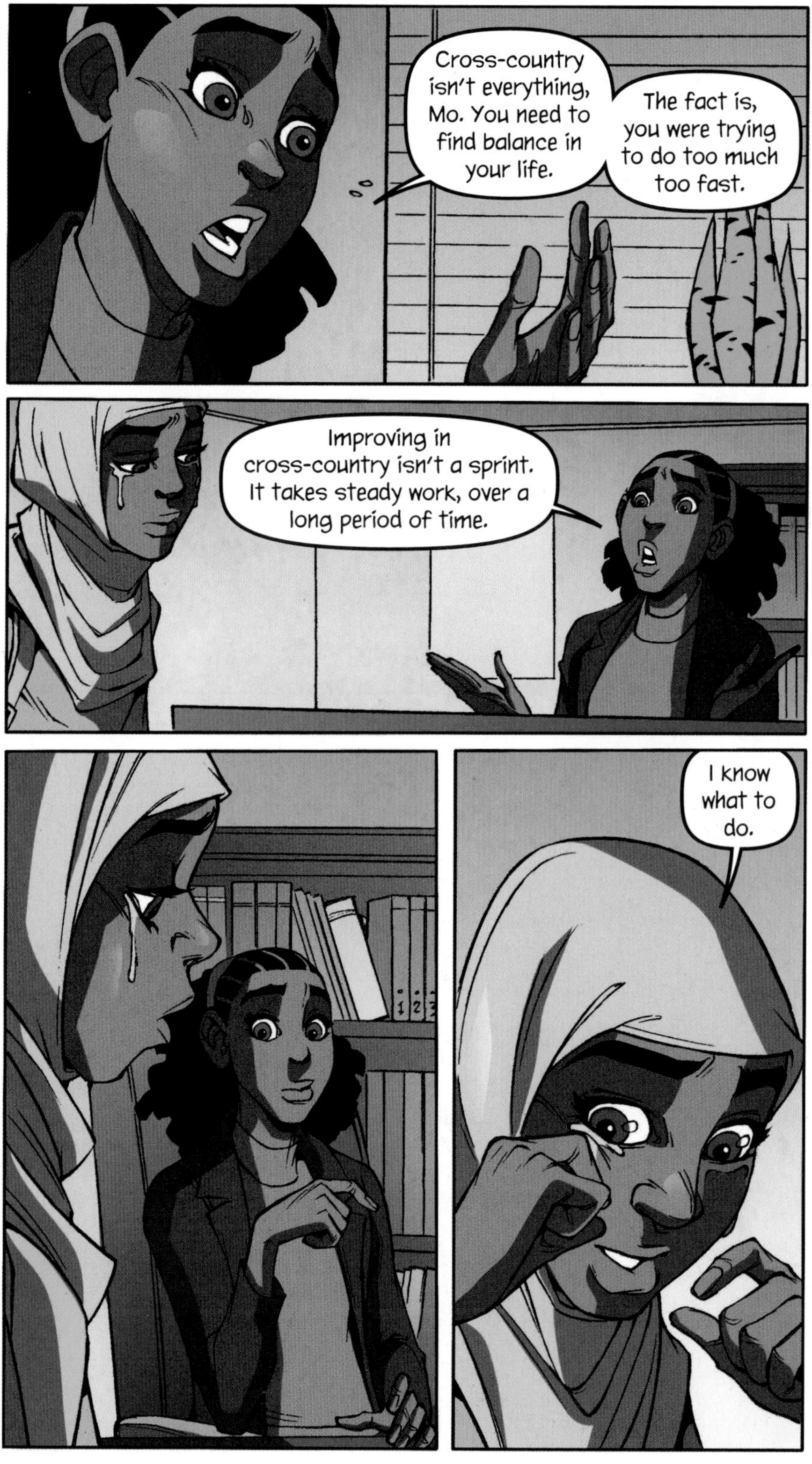
Cross-country isn't everything, Mo. You need to find balance in your life.
The fact is, you were trying to do too much too fast.
Improving in cross-country isn't a sprint. It takes steady work, over a long period of time.
I know what to do.

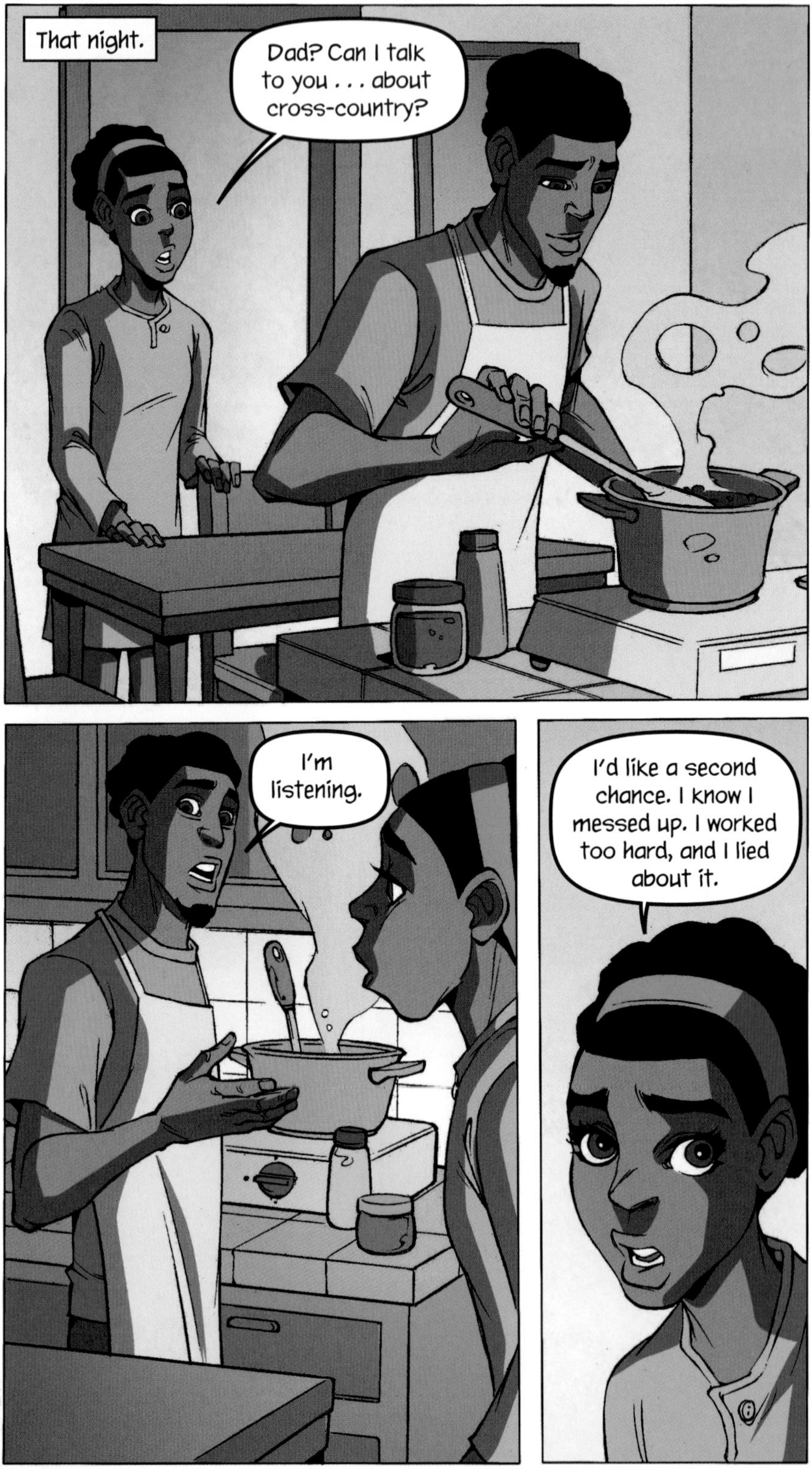
That night.
Dad? Can I talk to you . . . about cross-country?
I'm listening.
I'd like a second chance. I know I messed up. I worked too hard, and I lied about it.

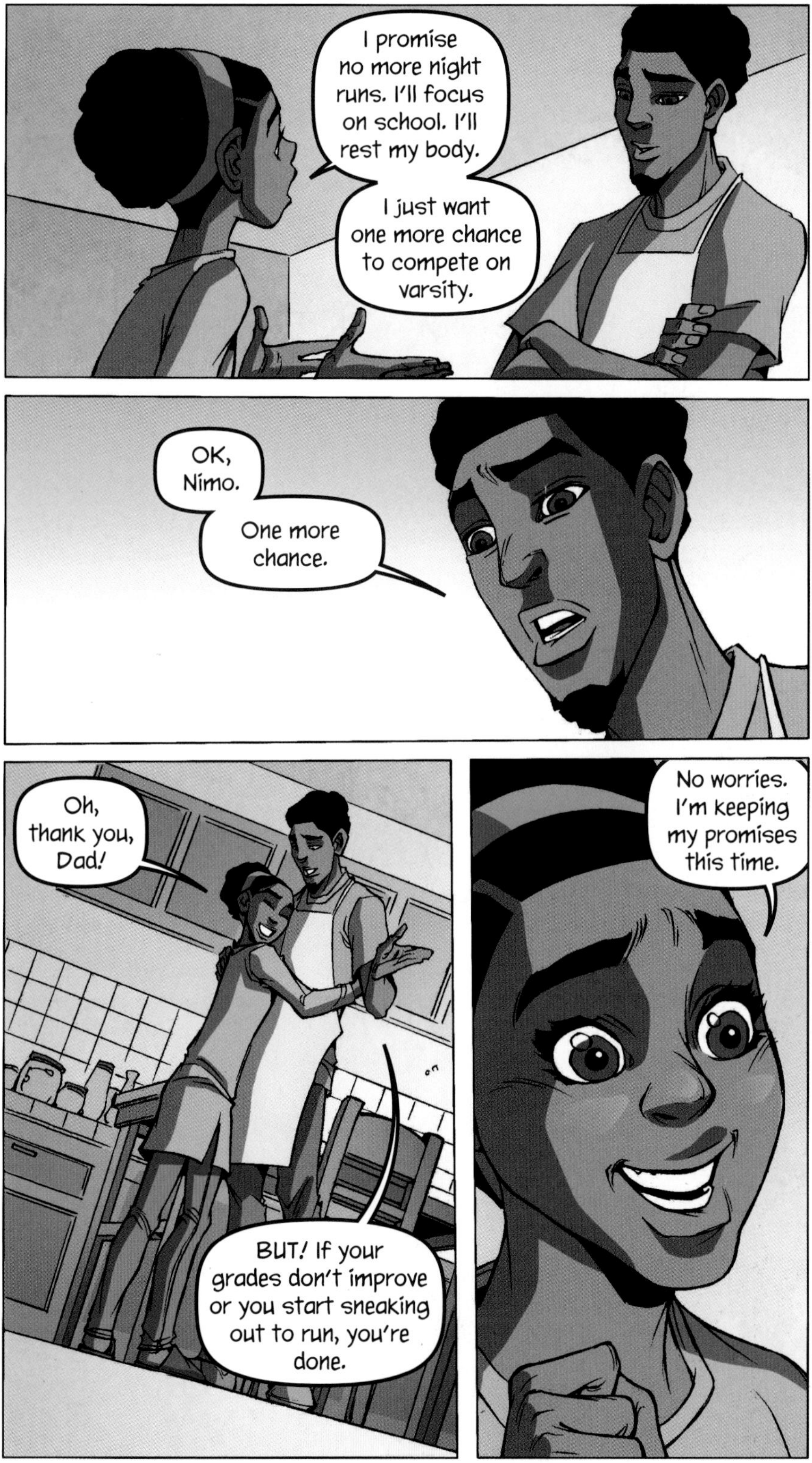
I promise no more night runs. I'll focus on school. I'll rest my body.
I just want one more chance to compete on varsity.
OK, Nimo.
One more chance.
Oh, thank you, Dad!
BUT! If your grades don't improve or you start sneaking out to run, you're done.
No worries. I'm keeping my promises this time.

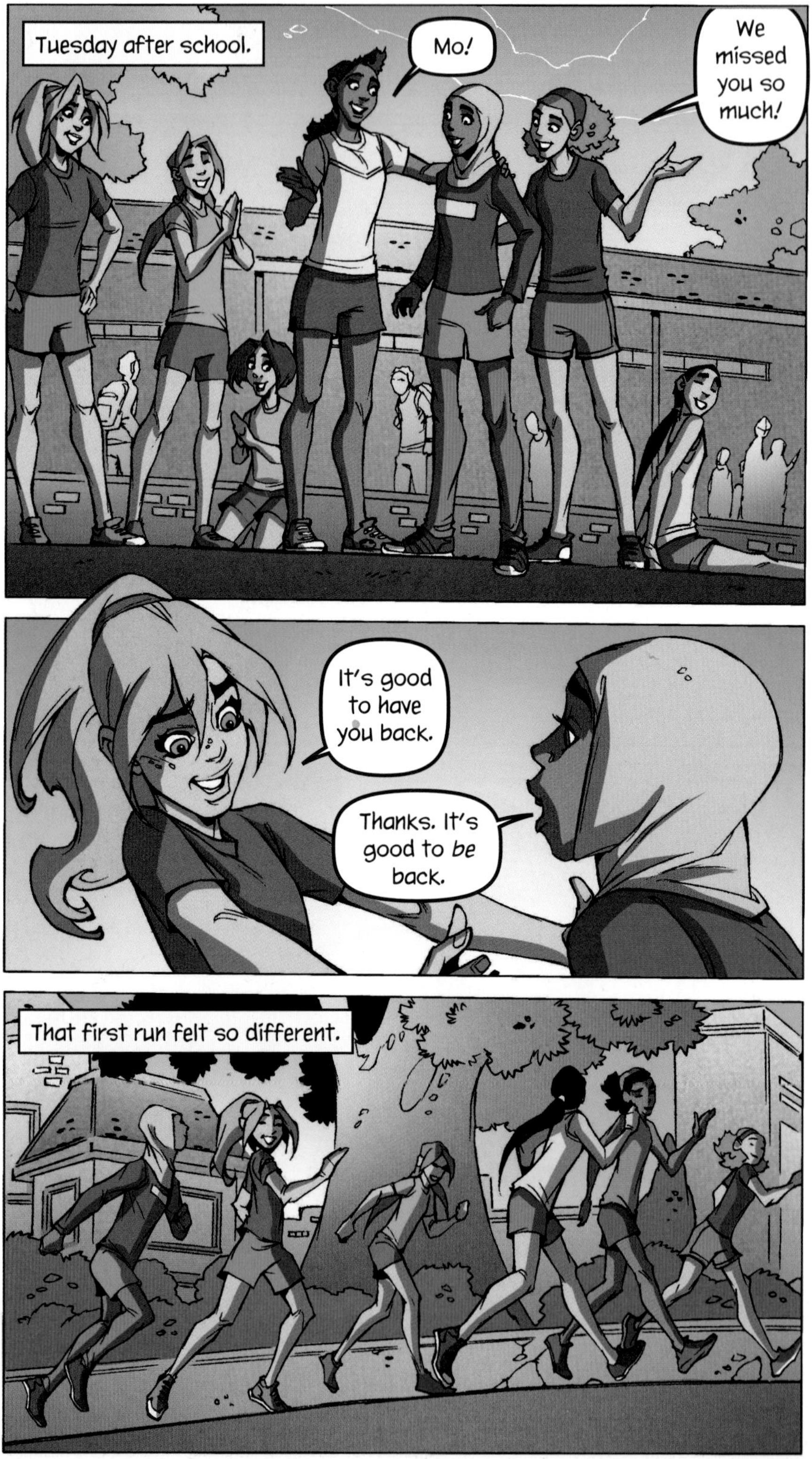
Tuesday after school.
Mo!
We missed you so much!
It's good to have you back.
Thanks. It's good to *be* back.
That first run felt so different.

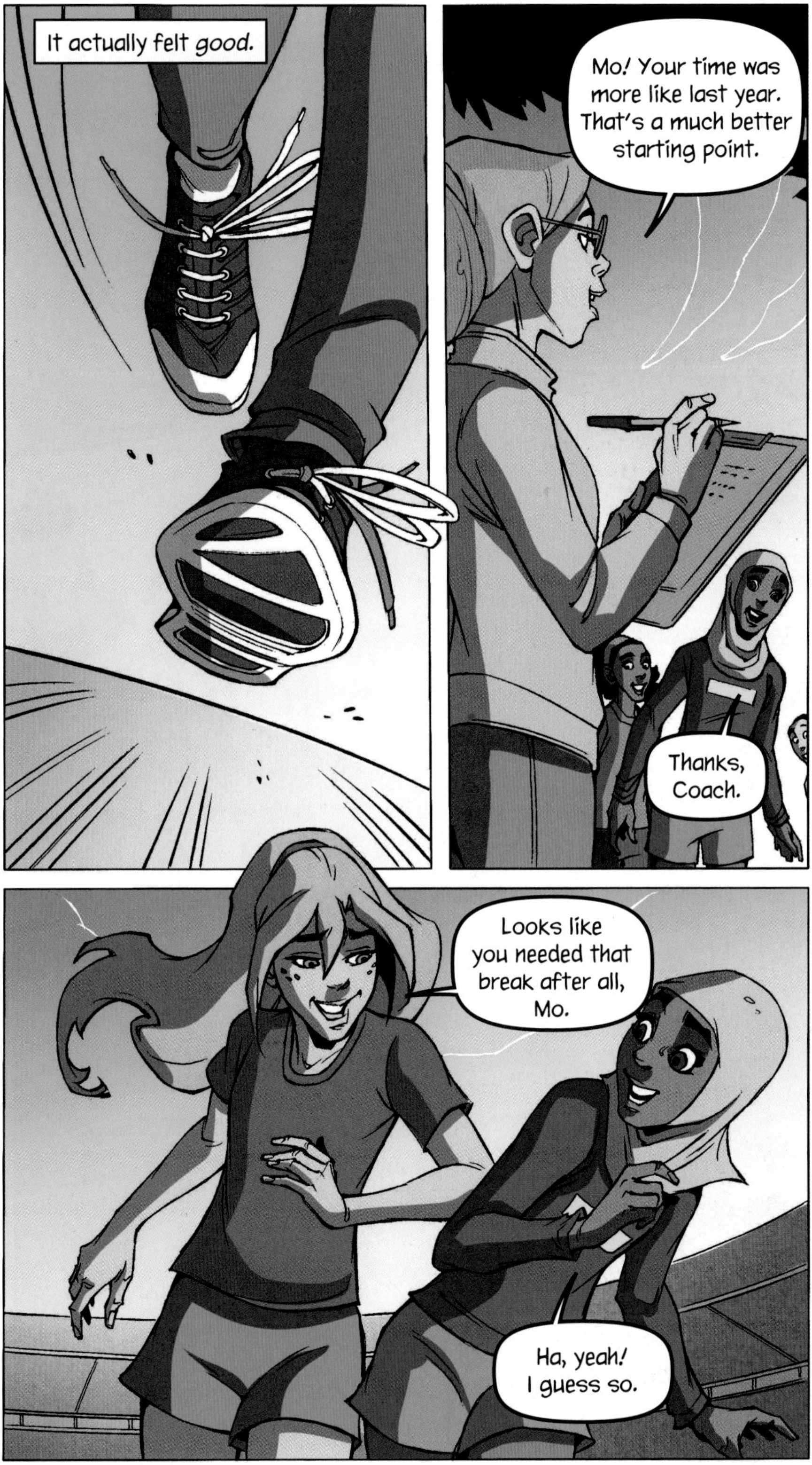
It actually felt *good.*
Mo! Your time was more like last year. That's a much better starting point.
Thanks, Coach.
Looks like you needed that break after all, Mo.
Ha, yeah! I guess so.

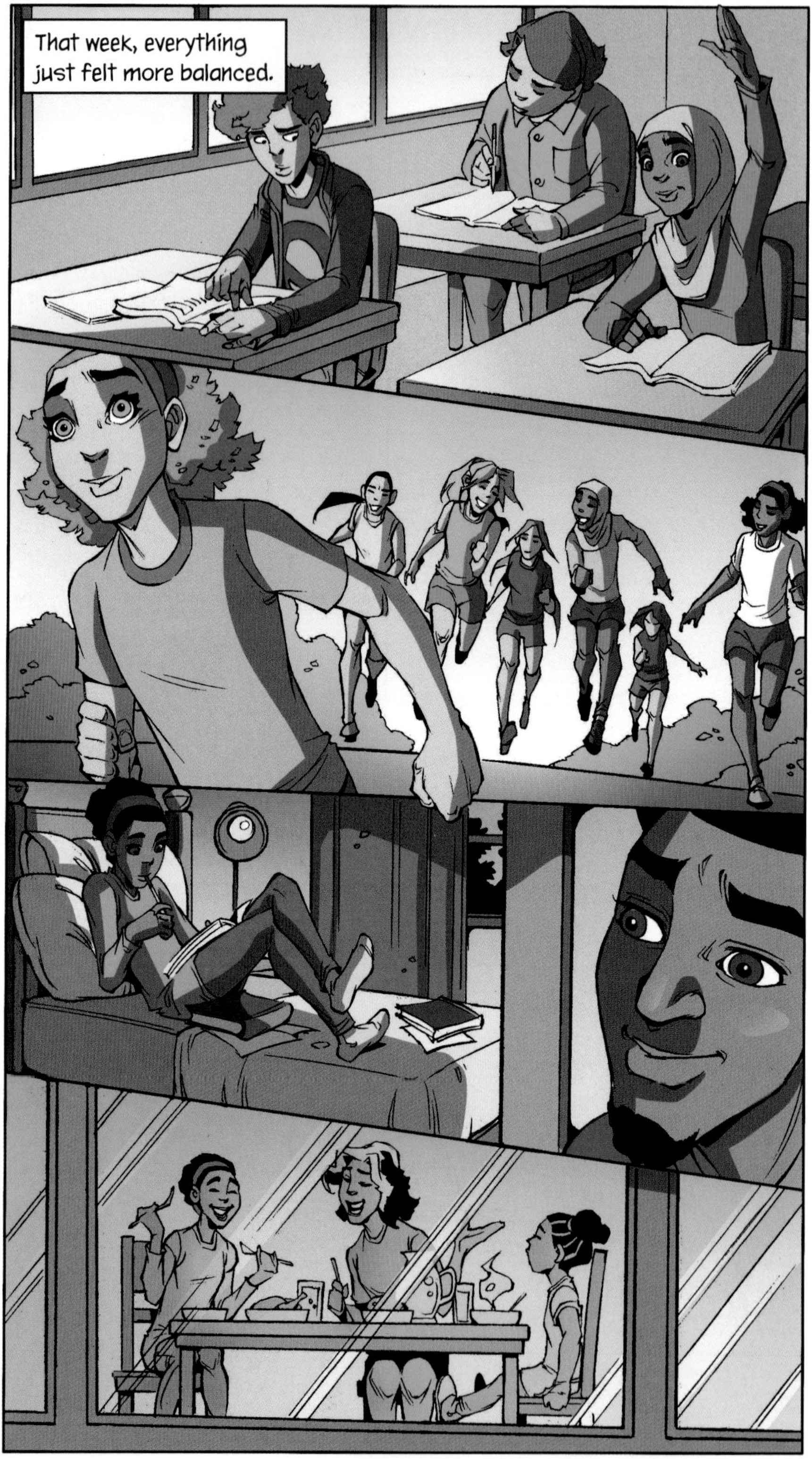
That week, everything just felt more balanced.

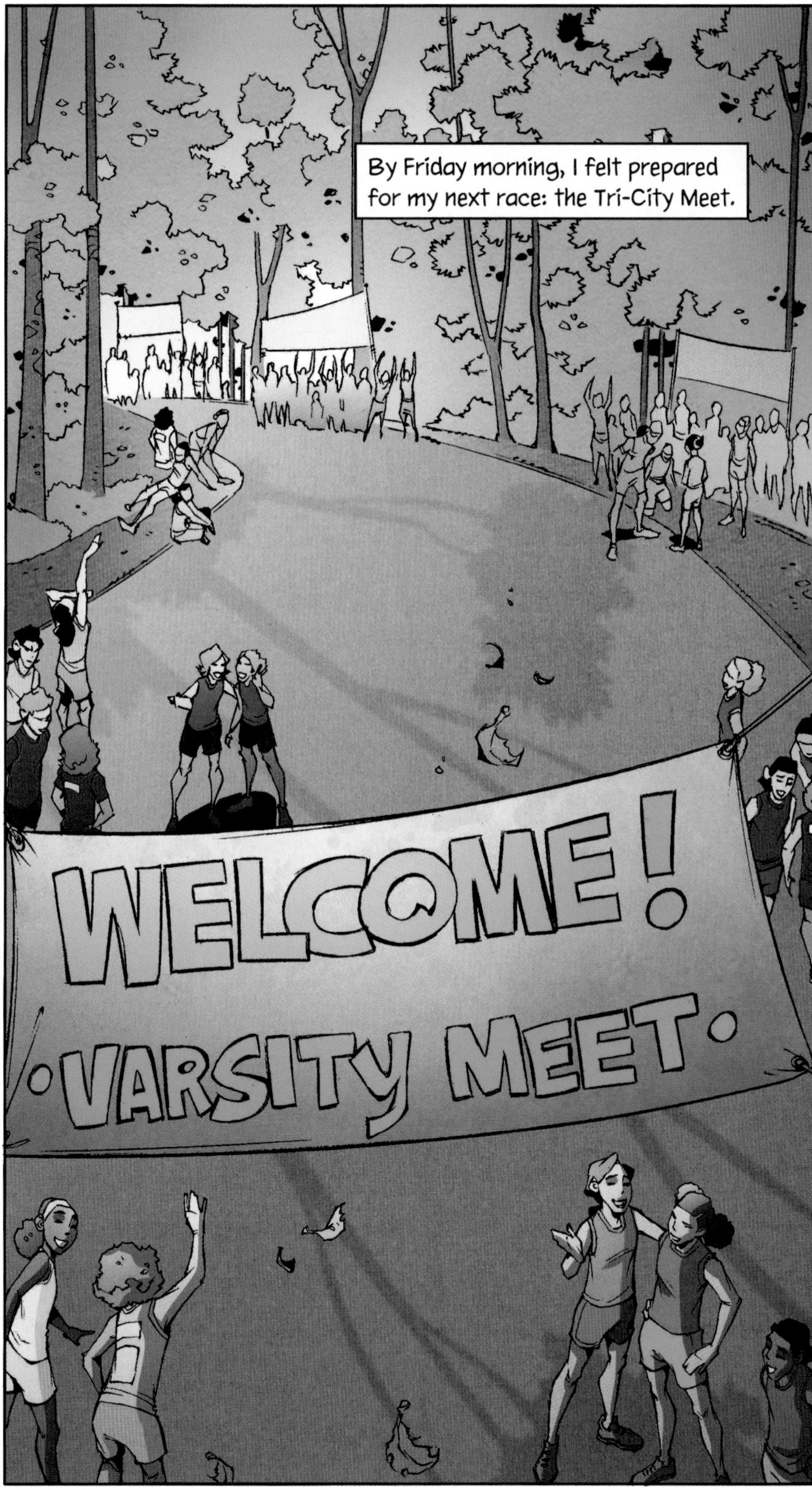
By Friday morning, I felt prepared for my next race: the Tri-City Meet.
WELCOME!
VARSITY MEET

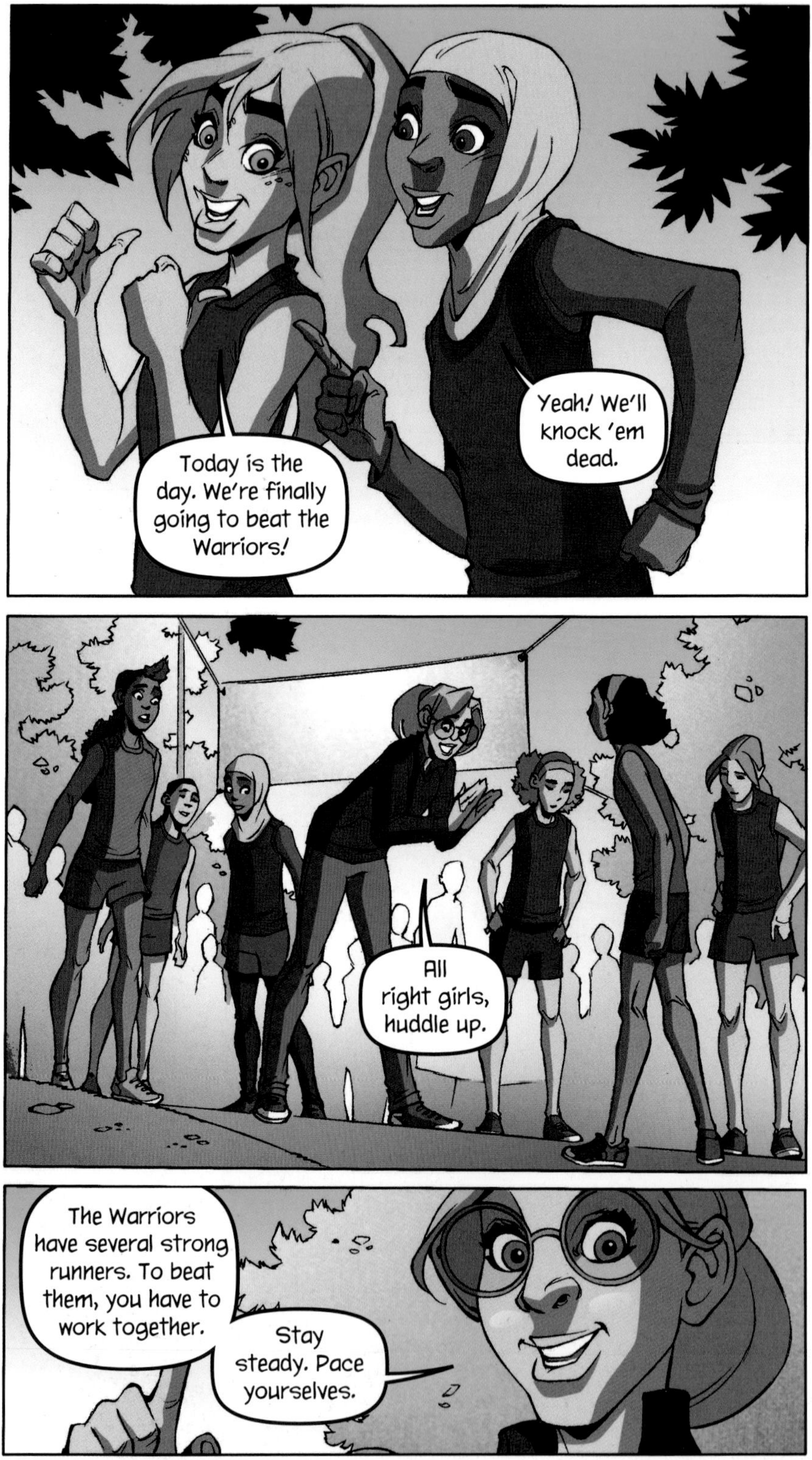
Today is the day. We're finally going to beat the Warriors!
Yeah! We'll knock 'em dead.
All right girls, huddle up.
The Warriors have several strong runners. To beat them, you have to work together.
Stay steady. Pace yourselves.

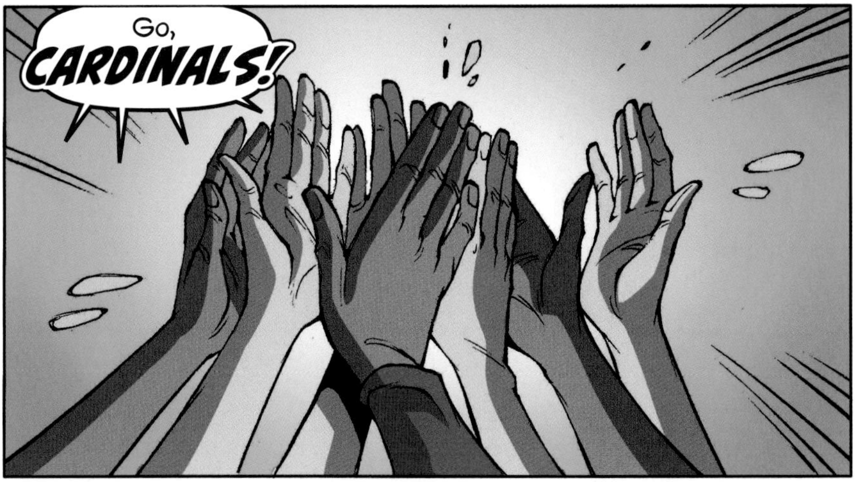
Go, CARDINALS!

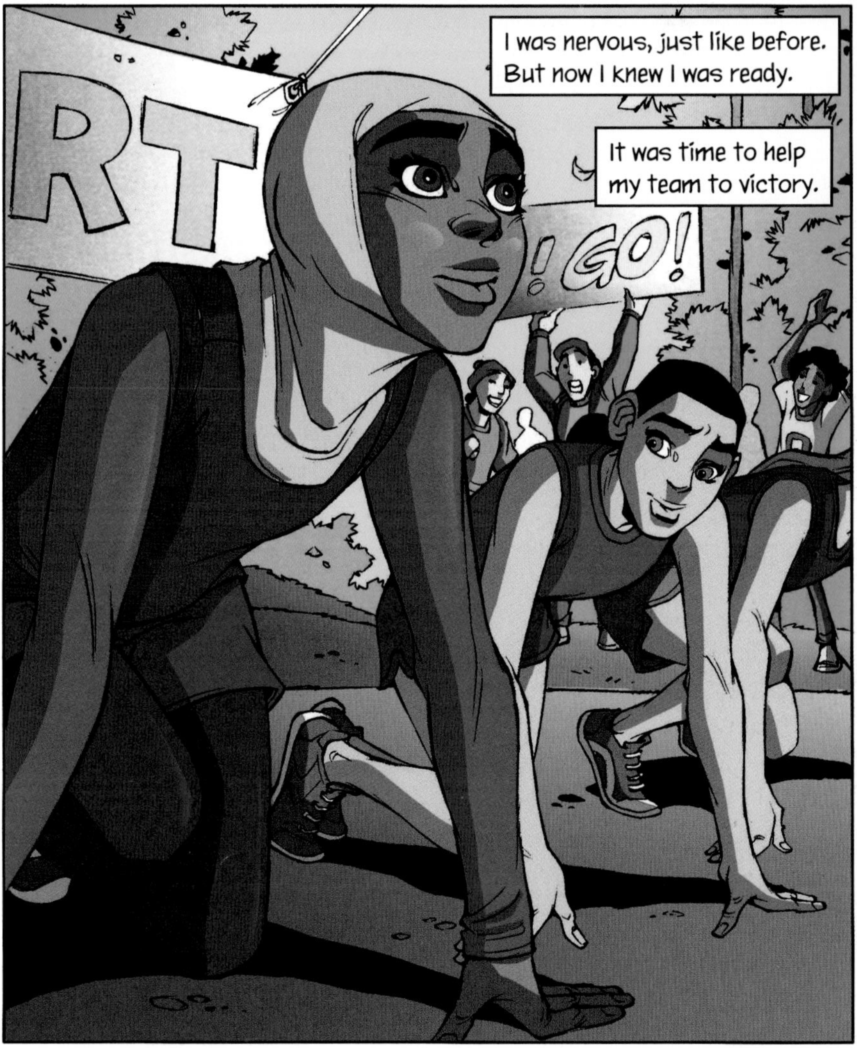
I was nervous, just like before. But now I knew I was ready.
It was time to help my team to victory.
GO!

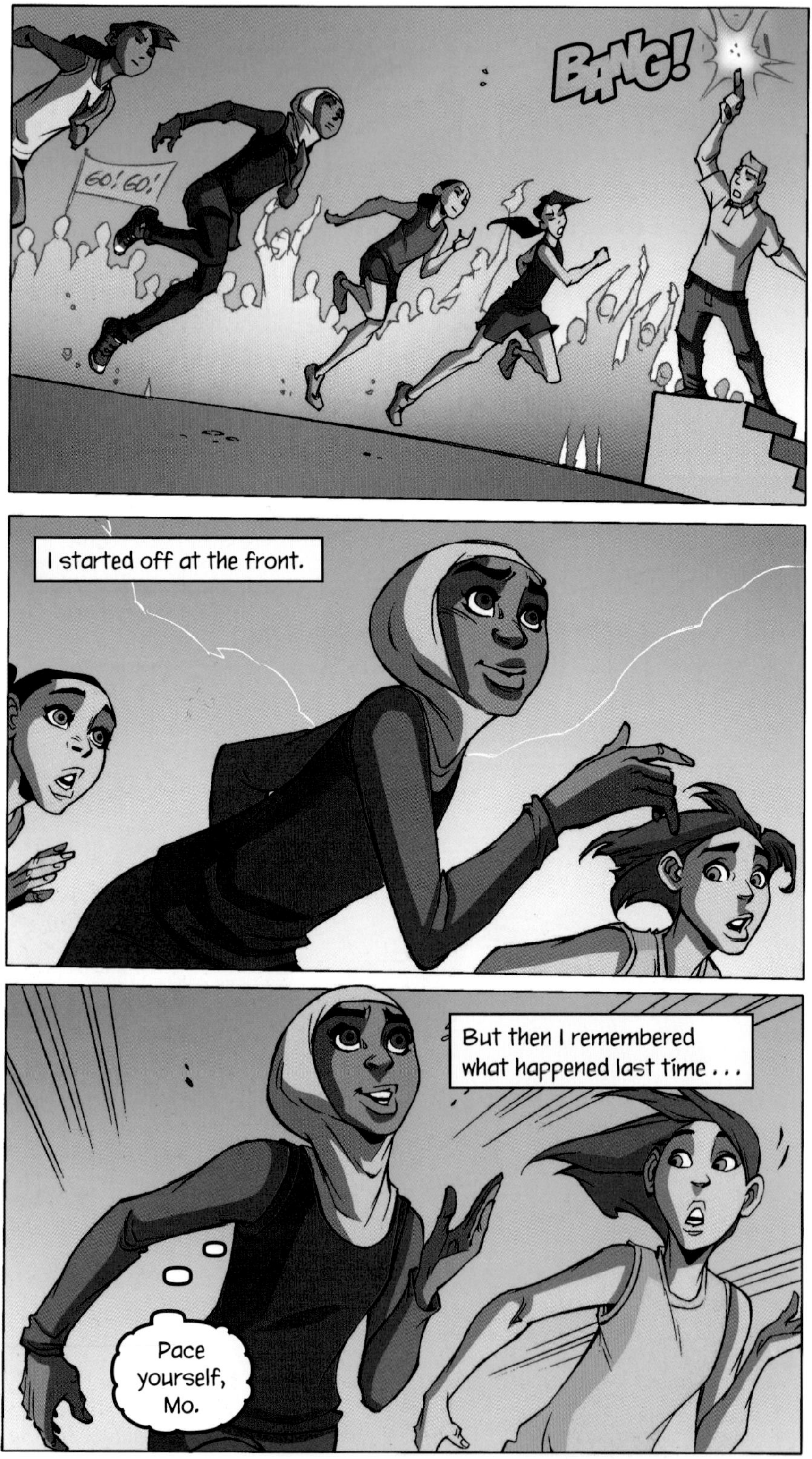
BANG!
GO! GO!
I started off at the front.
But then I remembered what happened last time . . .
Pace yourself, Mo.

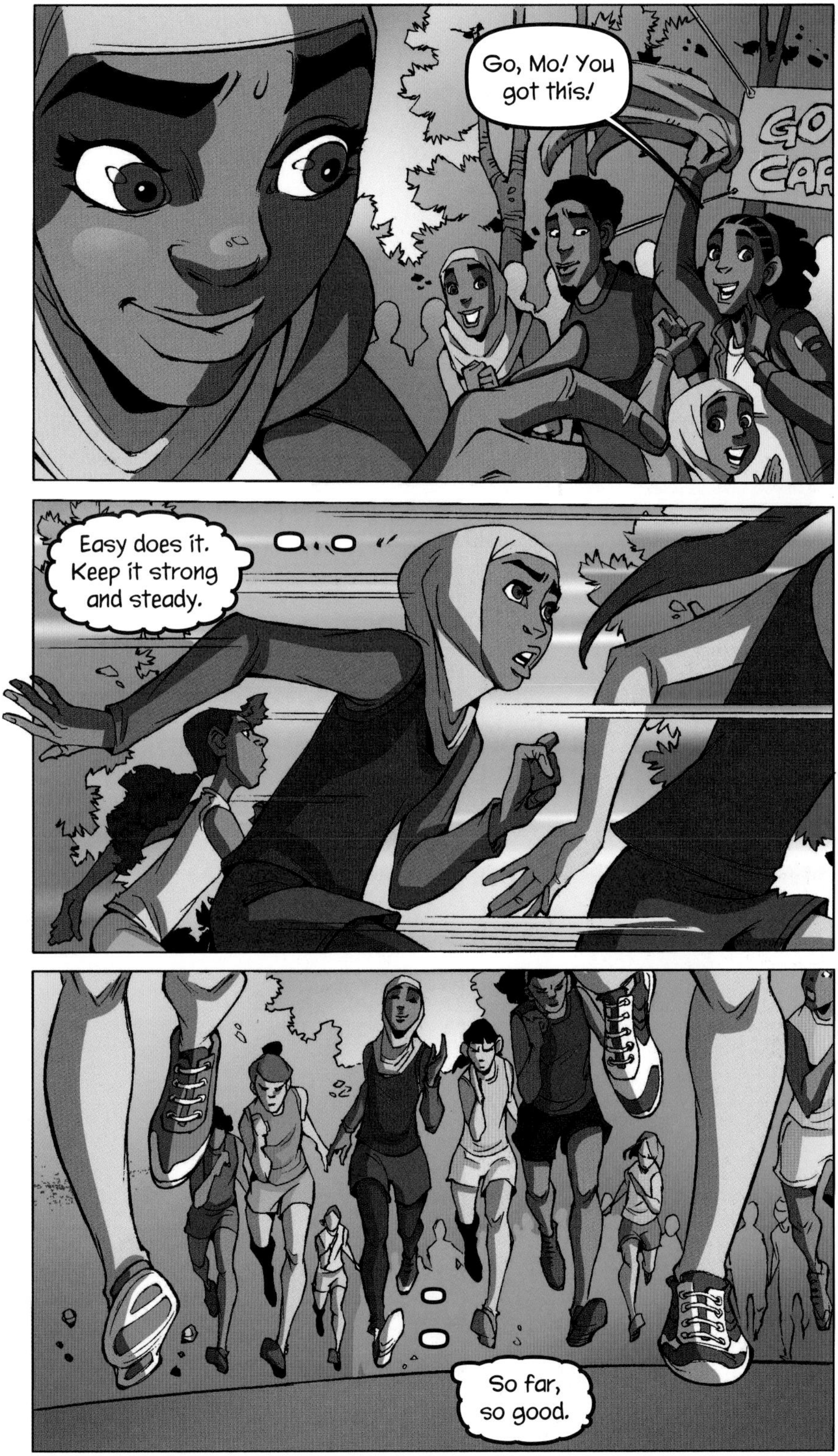
Go, Mo! You got this!
Easy does it. Keep it strong and steady.
So far, so good.

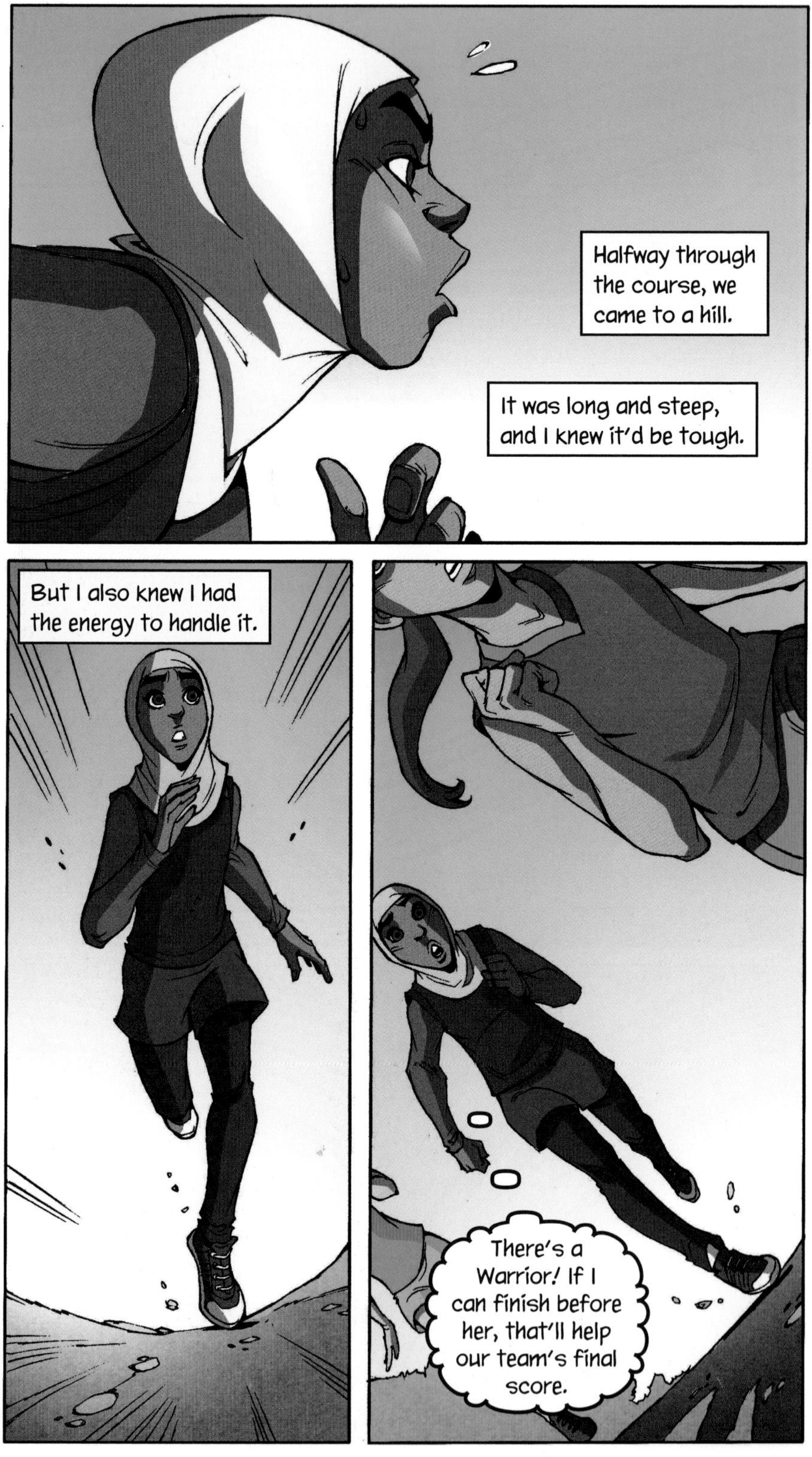
Halfway through the course, we came to a hill.
It was long and steep, and I knew it'd be tough.
But I also knew I had the energy to handle it.
There's a Warrior! If I can finish before her, that'll help our team's final score.

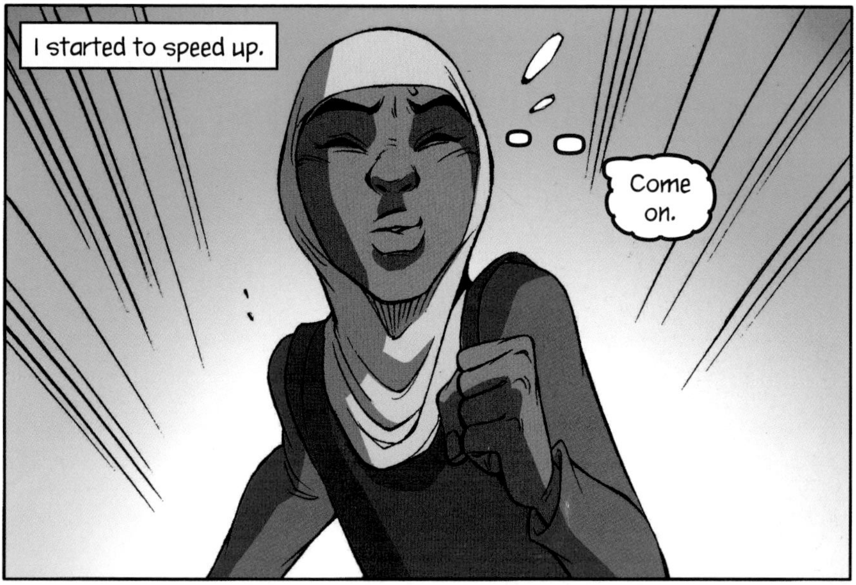
I started to speed up.
Come on.

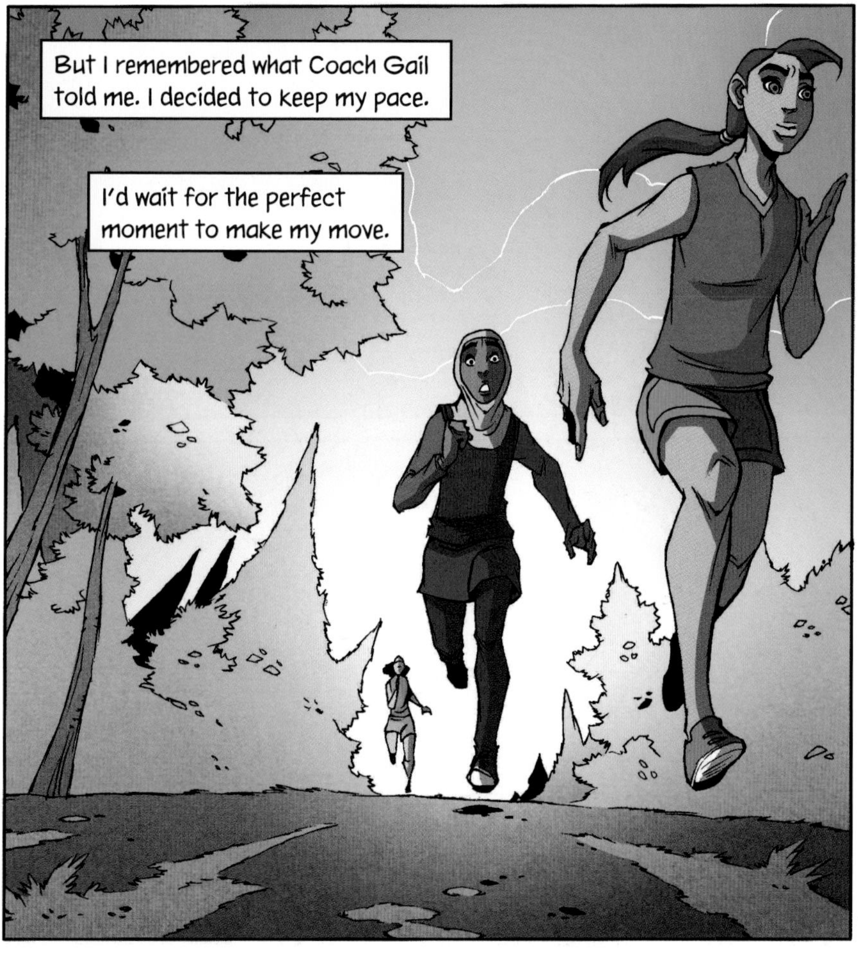
But I remembered what Coach Gail told me. I decided to keep my pace.
I'd wait for the perfect moment to make my move.

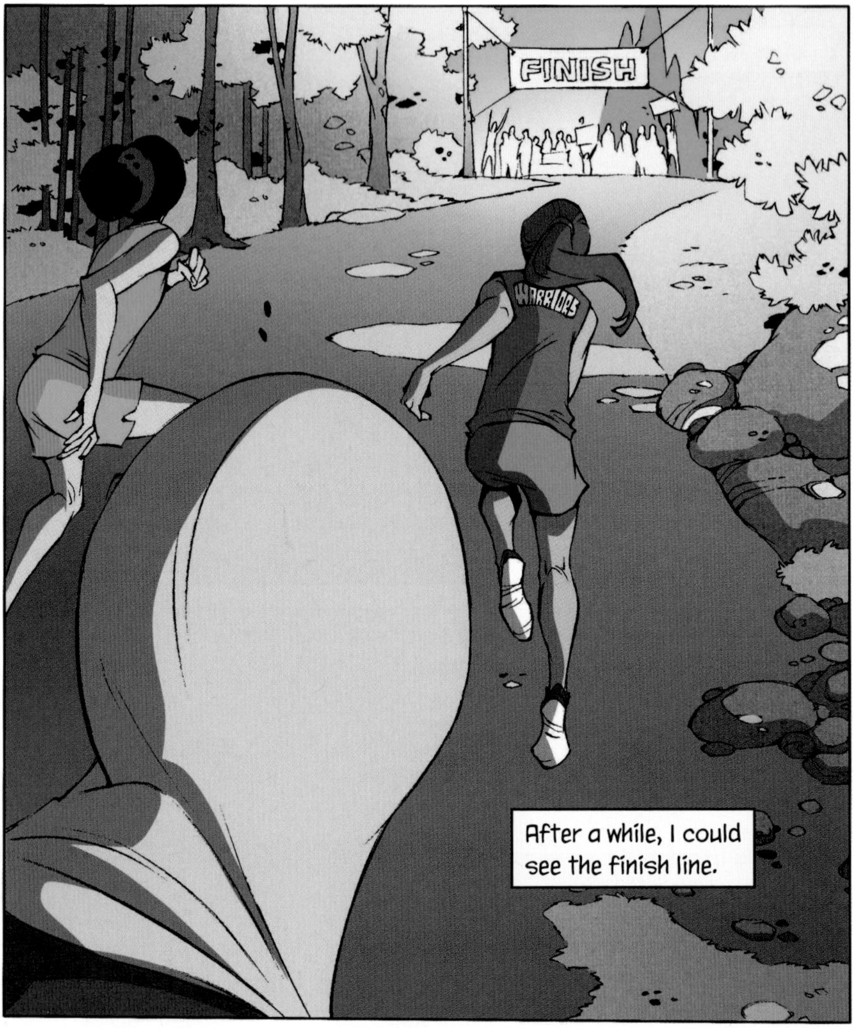
FINISH
WARRIORS
After a while, I could see the finish line.

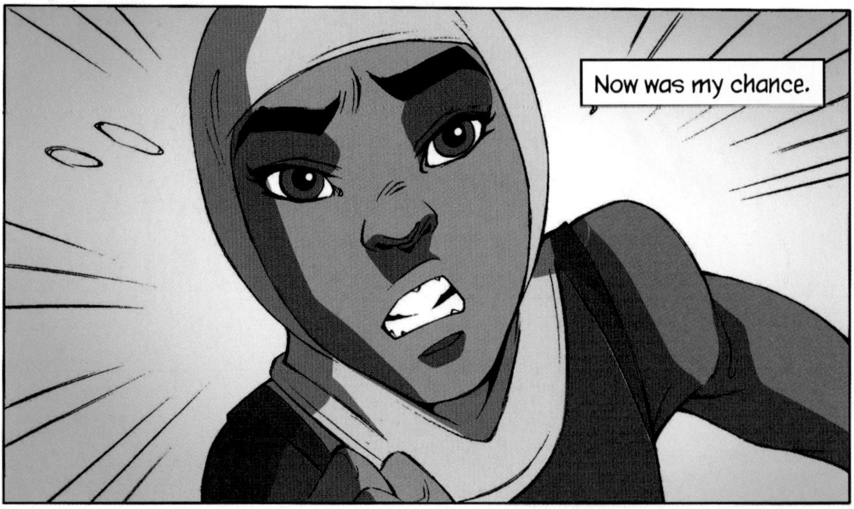
Now was my chance.

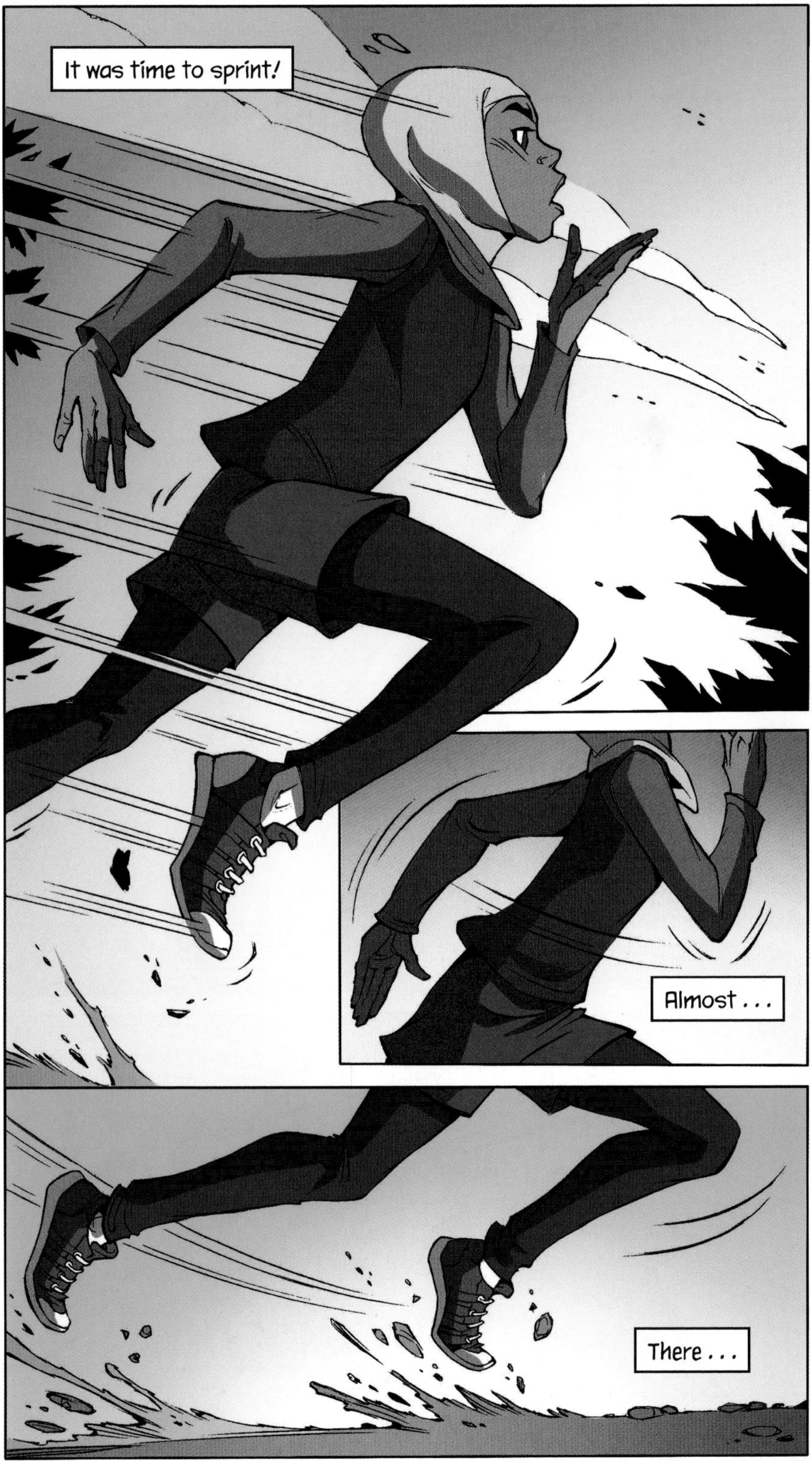
It was time to sprint!
Almost . . .
There . . .

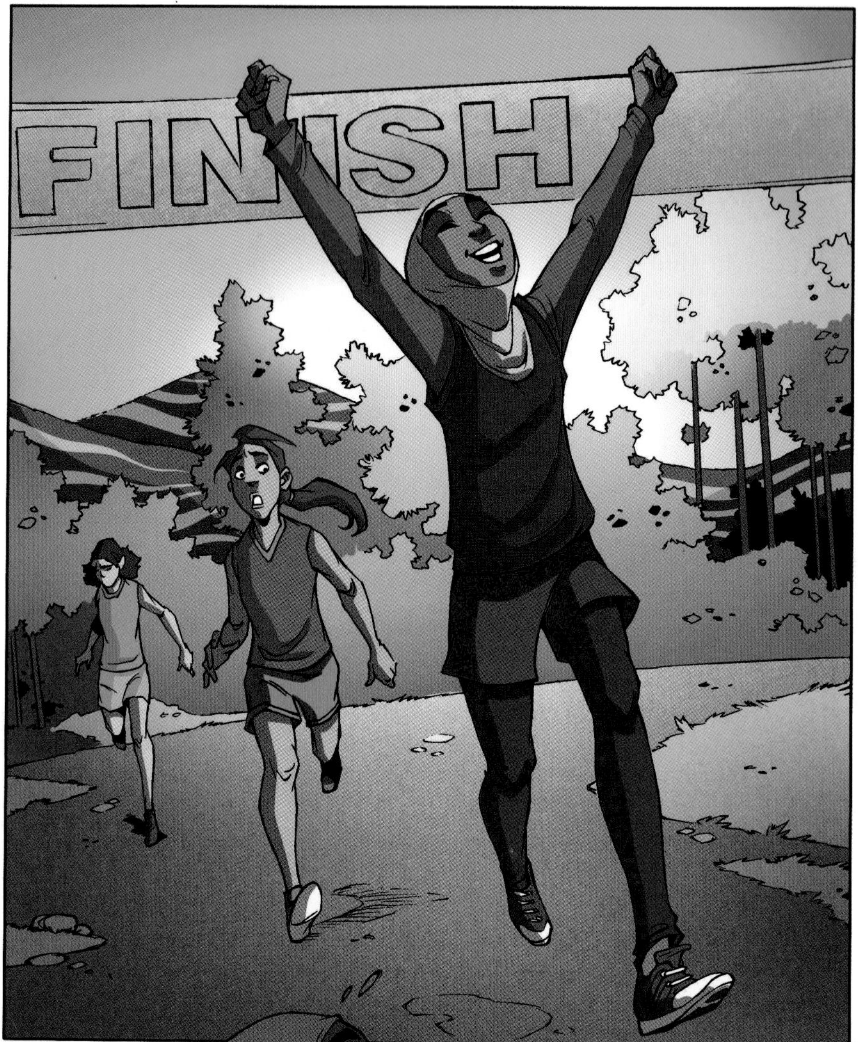
FINISH

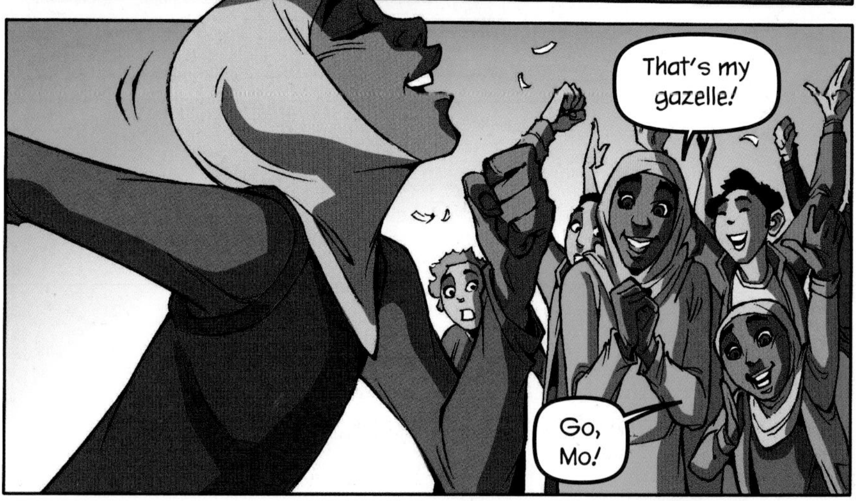
That's my gazelle!
Go, Mo!

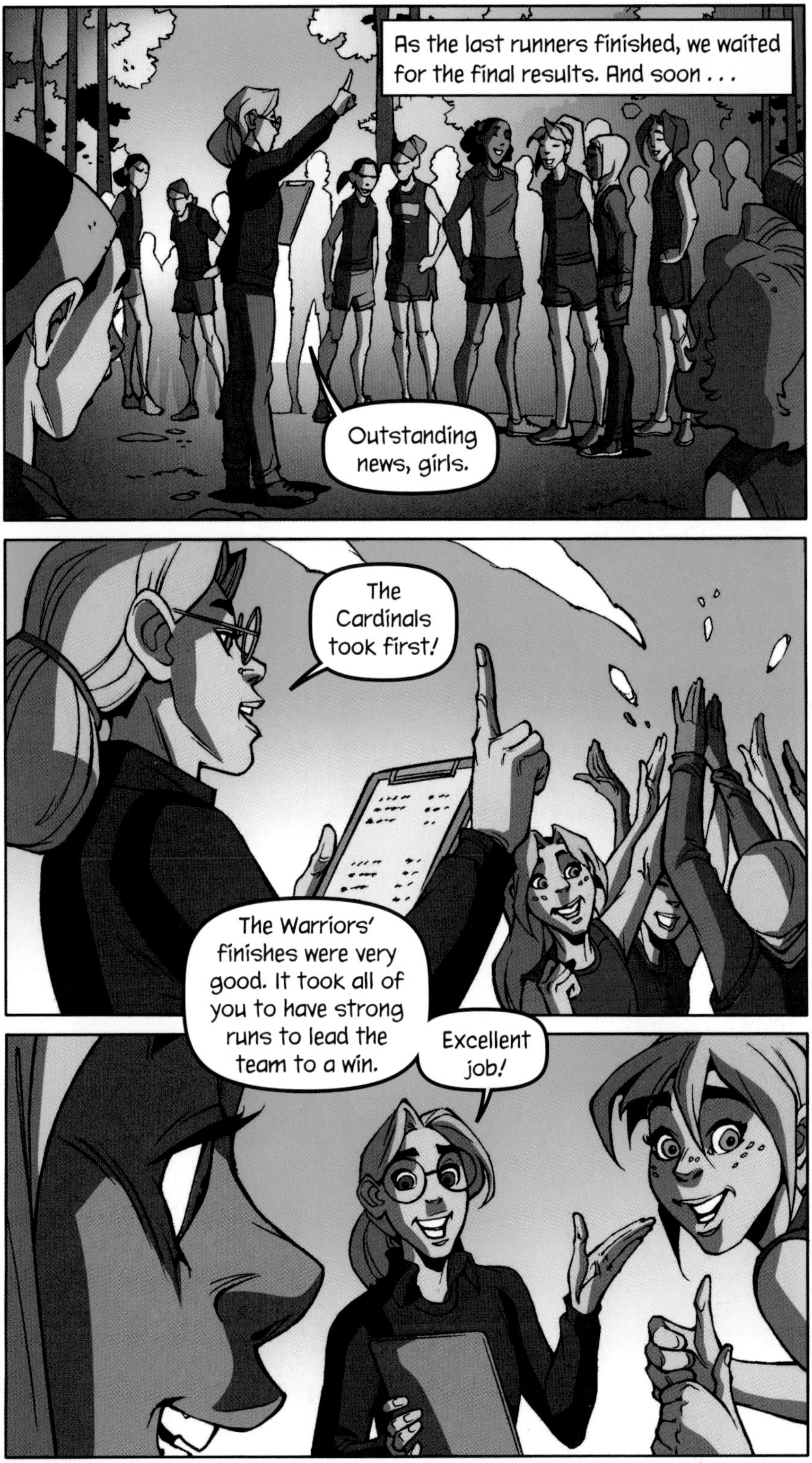
As the last runners finished, we waited for the final results. And soon . . .
Outstanding news, girls.
The Cardinals took first!
The Warriors' finishes were very good. It took all of you to have strong runs to lead the team to a win.
Excellent job!

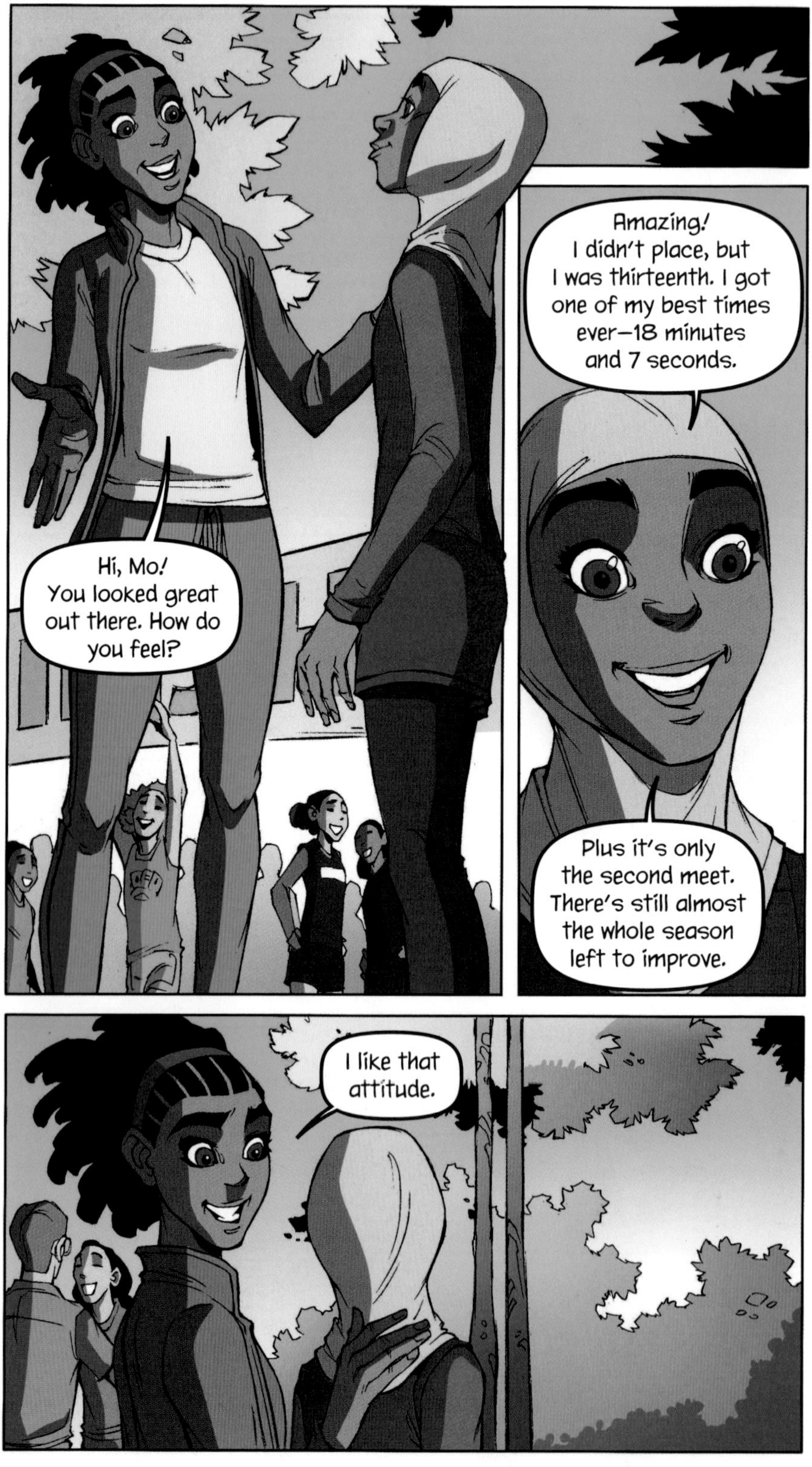
Hi, Mo! You looked great out there. How do you feel?
Amazing! I didn't place, but I was thirteenth. I got one of my best times ever—18 minutes and 7 seconds.
Plus it's only the second meet. There's still almost the whole season left to improve.
I like that attitude.

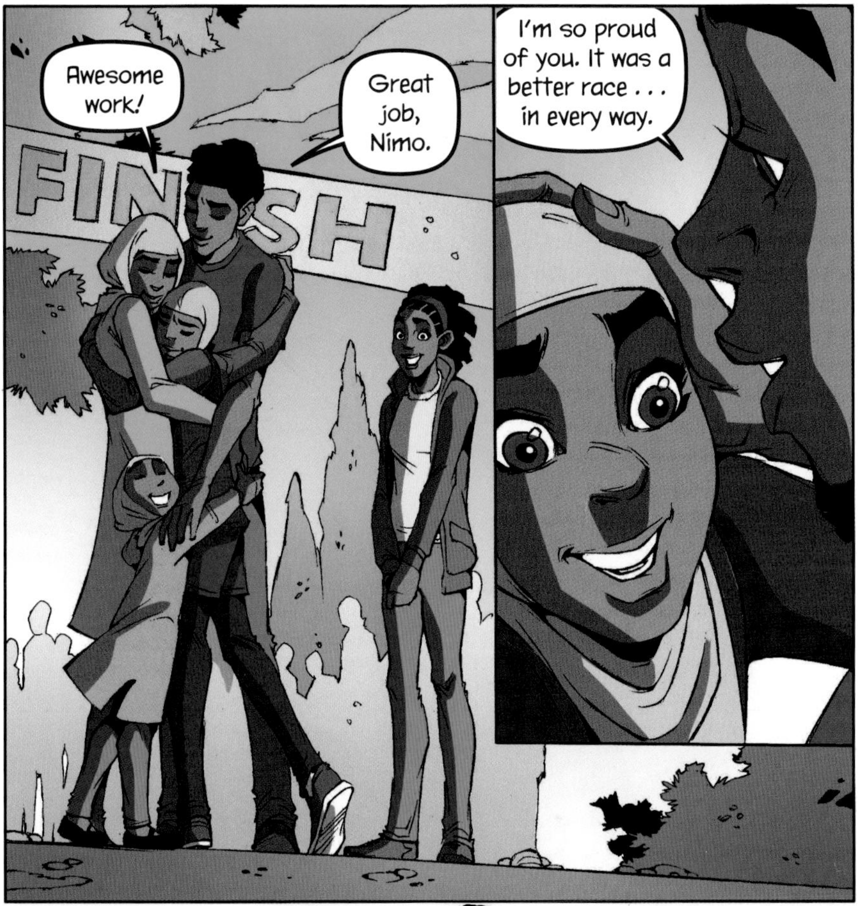
Awesome work!
Great job, Nimo.
FINISH
I'm so proud of you. It was a better race . . . in every way.

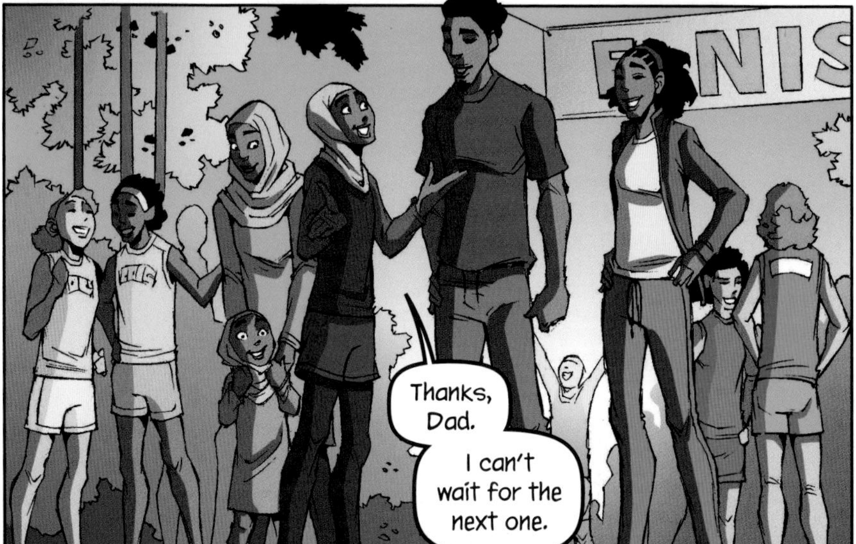
Thanks, Dad.
I can't wait for the next one.

VISUAL QUESTIONS

1. Nimo doesn't reply right away after her mom asks if she's allowed to go on extra runs. Why? What do you think is going through Nimo's mind? Why did the author decide to draw out this moment over two panels?

Uh . . .

Yeah. Of course!

2. There are no details in this panel on page 31. There is only Nimo and a purple background. What mood does this create? How does it connect to Nimo's feelings at this moment?

I had finished dead last.

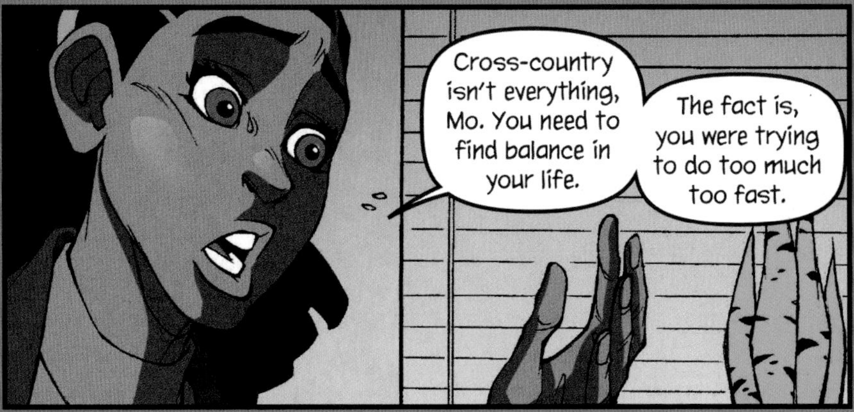
Cross-country isn't everything, Mo. You need to find balance in your life.
The fact is, you were trying to do too much too fast.

3. Both Nimo's dad and Coach Gail warn Nimo about running too much. Flip through the story and find three examples of how Nimo's extra runs affected her daily life. Be sure to look at both the text and art.

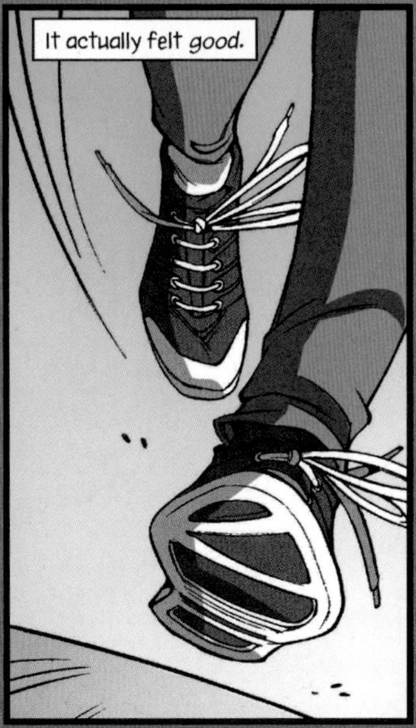
It actually felt *good*.

4. Creators of graphic novels decide what to show and not show in each panel. This is called framing. Why do you think the creators chose to show only Nimo's feet on page 51?

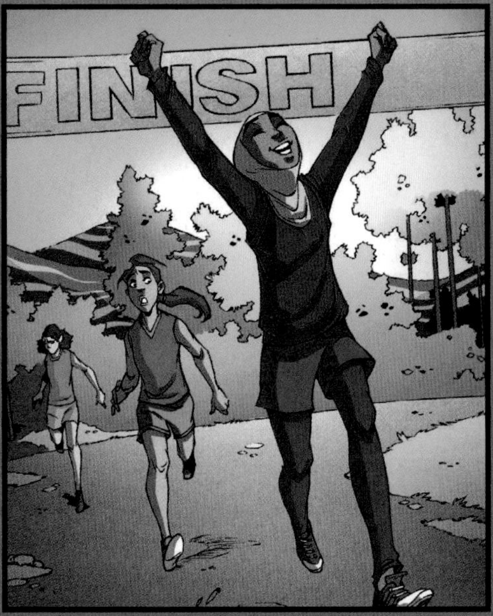
FINISH

5. On page 62, the first panel has no text, but the art still gives you lots of info. Describe what has just happened in the race. How do you think Nimo feels? How does this finish compare to her first meet?

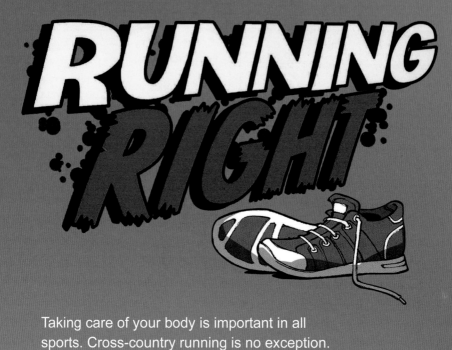

RUNNING RIGHT

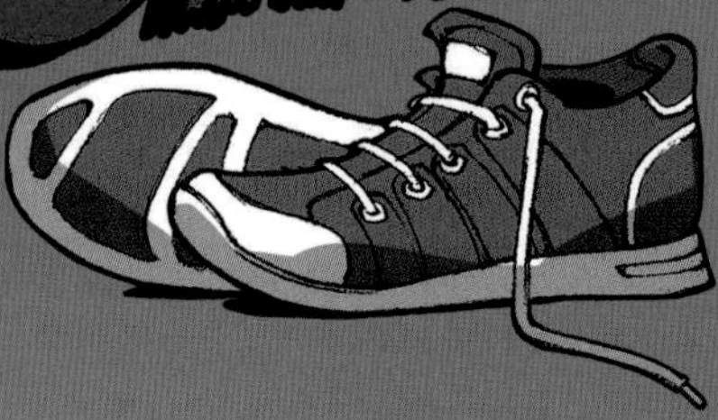

Taking care of your body is important in all sports. Cross-country running is no exception. Read on for tips on enjoying a long jog in a safe and healthy way!

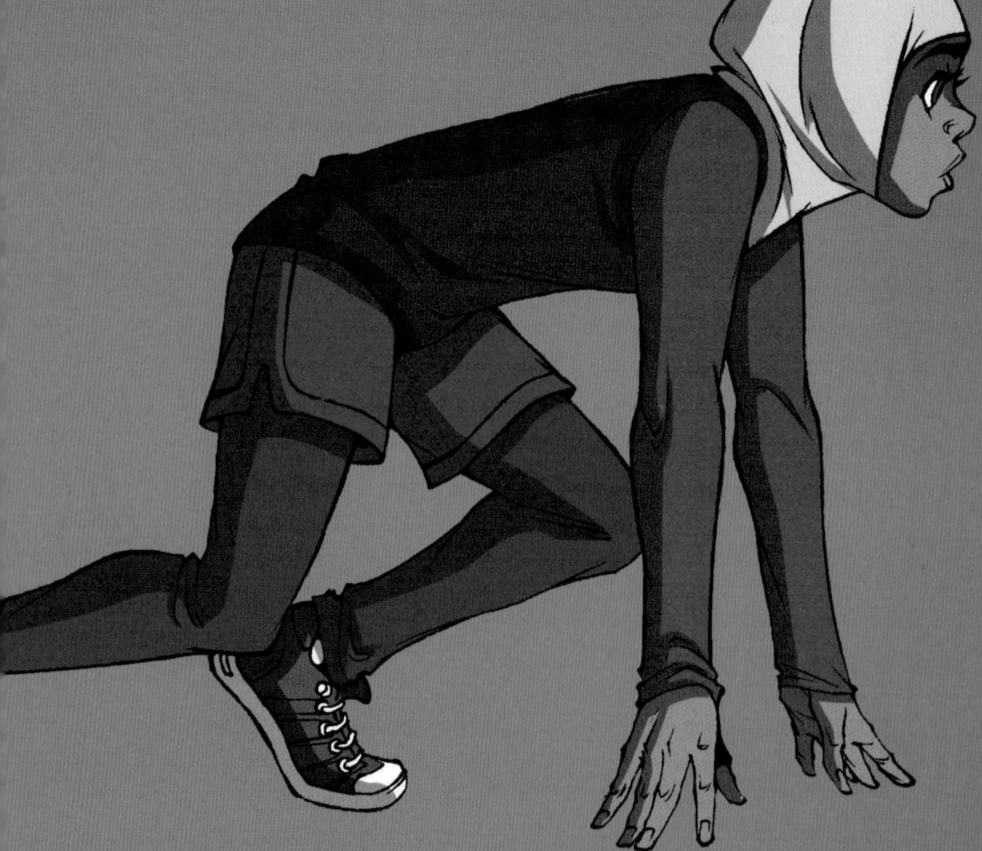

BEFORE YOU RUN

- **Eat right.** Cross-country runners need lots of whole grains, leafy greens, and lean proteins. These foods provide the energy to keep going for long distances.
- **Drink water.** Taking in enough water helps stop muscle cramps from happening.
- **Wear the right shoes.** Cross-country shoes are different from other types of running shoes. Plus, each person's feet are unique. Talk to an expert who can help you choose shoes that will make injuries less likely.
- **Warm up.** Light exercises before you begin literally warm up your muscles. This helps prepare your body for more intense activity.

AFTER YOU RUN

- **Stretch.** While your muscles are still warm from exercising, go through some stretches. It will help improve your overall flexibility and may help prevent soreness.
- **Drink water—again!** Your body loses water through sweat. Drinking water after a run helps replace what you lost and helps your body cool down.
- **Ice your legs.** Putting ice on your muscles can help them feel less sore.
- **Rest.** Take time to recover the day after a big run. Light exercise or stretching is OK for keeping your body in motion. But taking a break from running helps you avoid injuries and overexertion.

GLOSSARY

accomplishment (uh-KOM-plish-muhnt)—something that has been done as the result of much practice and great skill

advice (ad-VAHYS)—an opinion or suggestion about what to do about a problem

course (KORS)—the path that athletes (such as runners, cyclists, and skiers) move along, especially in a race

energy (EH-nuhr-jee)—the strength to move and do things

exhausted (ig-ZAWS-ted)—very tired and unable to do anything more

guilty (GIL-tee)—feeling bad because you have done (or think you have done) something bad or wrong

hit the wall—in running, to reach a point where you are very tired and it is difficult to keep going

improve (im-PROOV)—to make or become better

meet (MEET)—a large gathering where athletes (such as runners) take part in a race or a series of races

overexertion (oh-ver-eg-ZUR-shuhn)—an injury caused by doing the same motion too often or putting in too much effort at one time

pace (PAYSS)—to control the speed at which you do something; also, the speed at which you are moving

sprint (SPRINT)—to run at top speed for a short distance

steady (STED-ee)—staying the same over a long period of time

ABOUT THE AUTHOR

Connie R. Colwell is a writer, editor, and teacher. She studied writing at Concordia College in Moorhead, Minnesota, and went on to earn a Masters in Fine Arts in creative writing from Minnesota State University, Mankato. She has written over 100 books for kids on topics ranging from Marie Curie to the world's most disgusting foods. Today, she lives in Le Sueur, Minnesota, with her four children who all inspire her writing and keep her young at heart.

ABOUT THE ARTISTS

Tina Francisco is an artist from Bulacan, Philippines, and has only ever taken one drawing course in her entire life; she taught herself how to draw and tell a story. After a stint creating kids' comics in her native country, she became an in-demand animation storyboard artist. She joined Glass House Graphics nearly fifteen years ago and has since worked on a variety of projects, including Lost Kitties, Strawberry Shortcake, Casper, Knightingail, Megamind, and much more.

Jaymes Reed has operated the company Digital-CAPS: Comic Book Lettering since 2003. He has done lettering for many publishers, most notably Avatar Press. He's also the only letterer working with Inception Strategies, an Aboriginal-Australian publisher that develops social comics with public service messages for the Australian government. Jaymes is a 2012 and 2013 Shel Dorf Award Nominee.

Berenice Muñiz is a graphic designer and illustrator from Monterrey, Mexico. She has done work for publicity agencies, art exhibitions, and even created her own webcomic. These days, Berenice is devoted to illustrating comics as part of the Graphikslava crew.

READ THEM ALL!

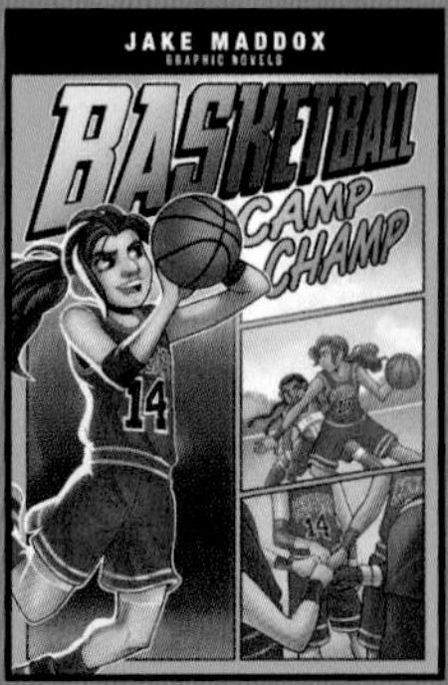
JAKE MADDOX
GRAPHIC NOVELS
BASKETBALL CAMP CHAMP

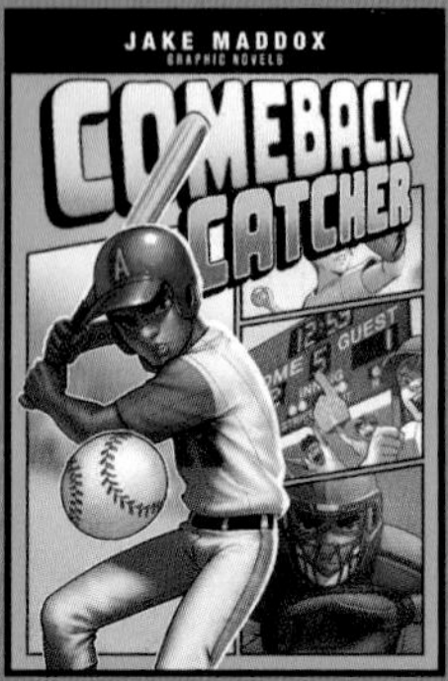
JAKE MADDOX
GRAPHIC NOVELS
COMEBACK CATCHER

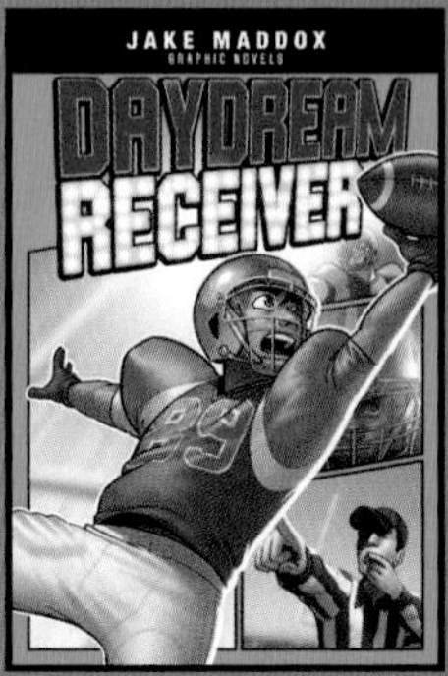
JAKE MADDOX
GRAPHIC NOVELS
DAYDREAM RECEIVER

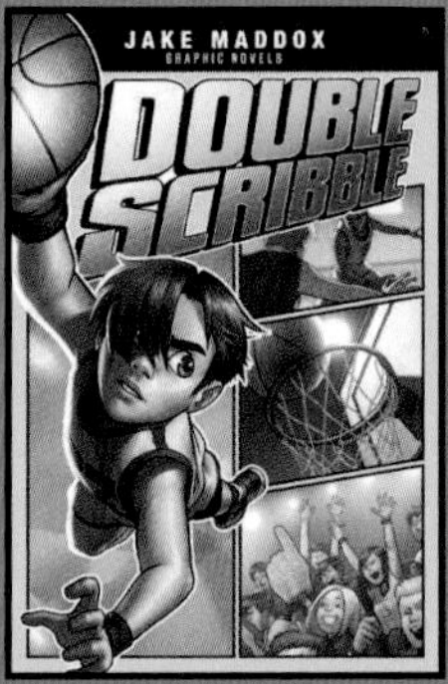
JAKE MADDOX
GRAPHIC NOVELS
DOUBLE SCRIBBLE

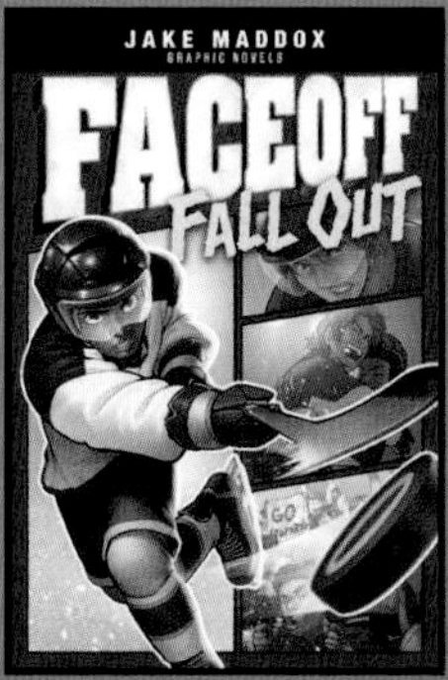
JAKE MADDOX
GRAPHIC NOVELS
FACEOFF FALL OUT

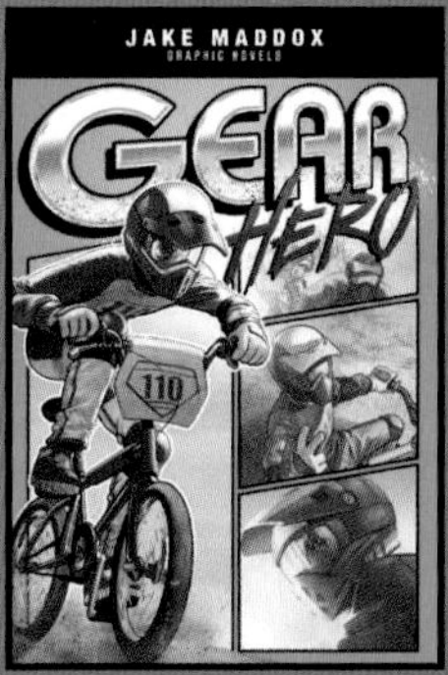
JAKE MADDOX
GRAPHIC NOVELS
GEAR HERO

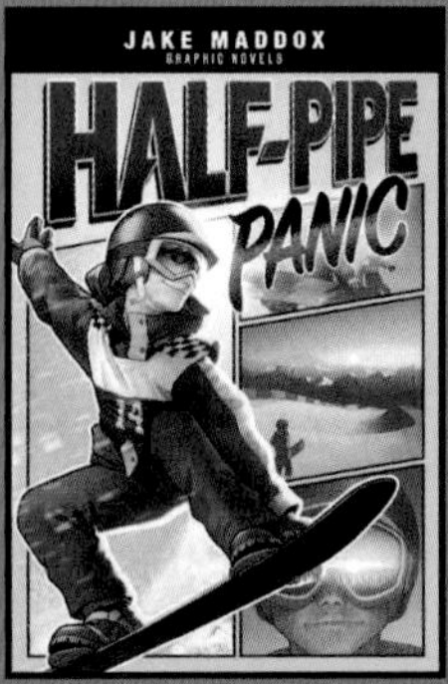
JAKE MADDOX
GRAPHIC NOVELS
HALF-PIPE PANIC

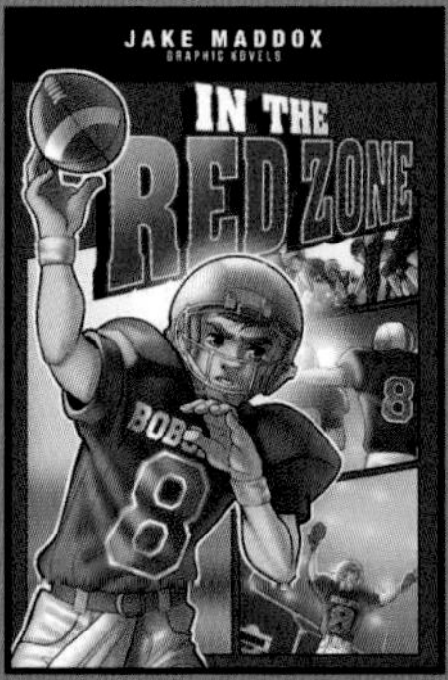
JAKE MADDOX
GRAPHIC NOVELS
IN THE RED ZONE

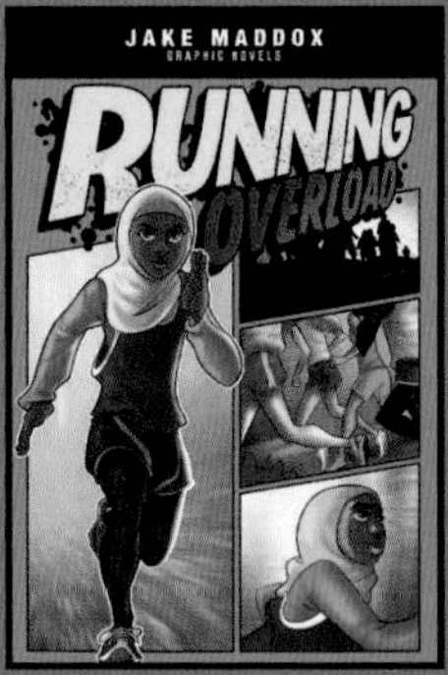
JAKE MADDOX
GRAPHIC NOVELS
RUNNING OVERLOAD

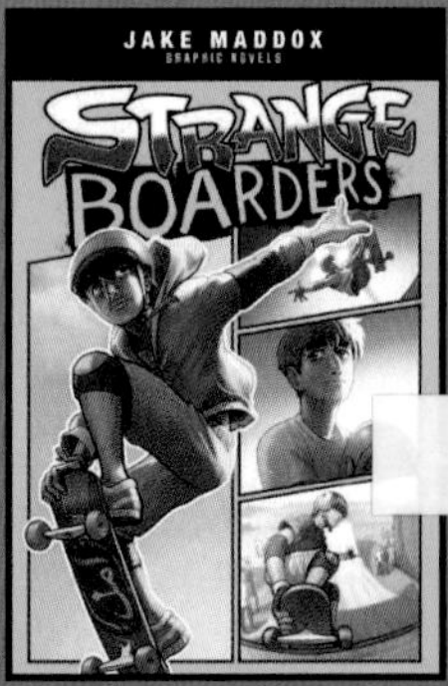
JAKE MADDOX
GRAPHIC NOVELS
STRANGE BOARDERS

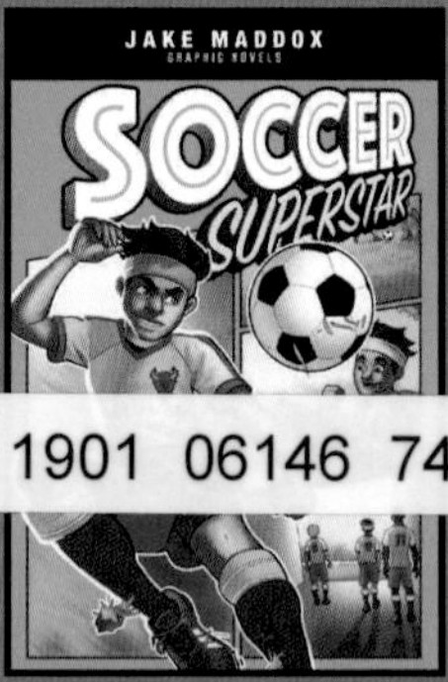
JAKE MADDOX
GRAPHIC NOVELS
SOCCER SUPERSTAR

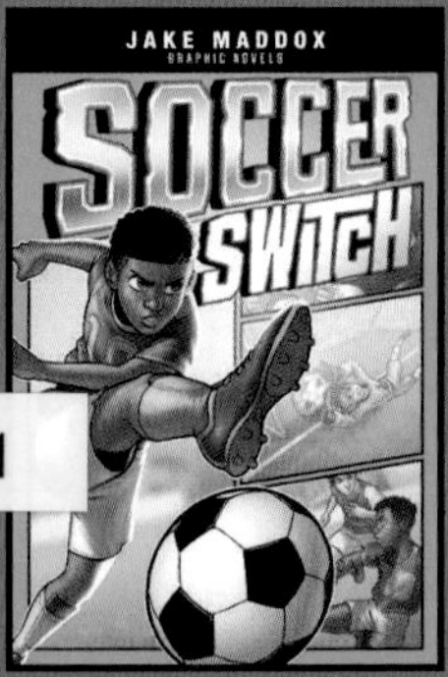
JAKE MADDOX
GRAPHIC NOVELS
SOCCER SWITCH